Escape to Kenya

Shannon Bernard

Chapter 1

Dream Come True

The bus lurched violently, jolting Claire awake. She gasped, her heart thundering as her eyes darted around.

What in the world...?

Another bone-rattling shudder ripped through the vehicle, shaking the floor beneath her feet. Before she could brace herself, a sharp turn flung her sideways, her head striking the grimy window beside her with a *thud*.

Claire let out a startled yelp, but it was drowned out by the boisterous shouts and laughter echoing from the front of the bus.

Disoriented, she blinked rapidly, her vision swimming as she squinted out the window, trying to make sense of the chaos.

The smooth pavement of Nairobi's highway had been replaced by a rugged dirt road, riddled with potholes deep enough to swallow the bus whole. The Kenyan countryside stretched out in all directions, endless grasslands broken only by the solitary silhouette of a distant tree.

Another brutal swerve nearly sent Claire flying from her seat. The bus groaned in protest, its suspension clearly long past its prime.

From her seat in the back, she cast a quick glance toward the passengers in the front rows. They sat calm and composed, chatting like they were lounging in a café—an infuriating contrast to her own rattled state.

How are they so unfazed? Are we even on the same bus?

Her gaze then darted to the driver—a weathered Kenyan man who maneuvered the bus with a calm that bordered on the supernatural. With deft precision, he zigzagged around protruding rocks, scurrying animals, and the occasional pedestrian without so much as a flinch.

For a fleeting moment, Claire was begrudgingly impressed.

Then, the bus struck a pothole the size of a small crater and bucked wildly.

She shrieked as she was catapulted into the air, limbs flailing before crashing back down into her seat, her elbow slamming into the young man beside her.

"Sorry about that," she mumbled, heat rushing into her cheeks.

"No worries," he replied cheerfully, rubbing his shoulder. "This road *is* a bit of a challenge, right?"

"Challenge?" she repeated, unable to keep the sarcasm from her voice. "That's one way to put it."

While the other passengers buzzed with excitement over glimpses of wildlife, Claire clung to the seat in front of her, unwilling, or unable, to share their enthusiasm.

She was normally the picture of composure, but now she felt like taut wire, one touch away from snapping. Her brown eyes darted anxiously between the gaping holes ahead and the seat inches from her knees.

Flustered and on edge, her usual optimism was crushed beneath every frustration that had dogged her since setting foot in Kenya.

The trouble had started when she landed and learned the airline had lost her luggage. Their empty promises to "locate it soon" had done little to soften the blow. Now, thousands of miles from home, she had nothing but the clothes on her back and the sparse contents of her leather backpack.

As if that weren't aggravating enough, the bus scheduled to pick up her group arrived two hours late. By the time she climbed aboard, the only available seats were the cramped, uncomfortable ones at the very back.

Regret settled deep in her chest, twisting with a bitter edge. Had coming to Kenya been a terrible mistake?

At first, the idea of spending her last semester of college in Africa seemed like a dream come true. She saw it as an opportunity to immerse herself in a land rich with diverse cultures and ancient mysteries. It promised to be a once-in-a-lifetime experience she couldn't resist.

While most of her peers gravitated toward the larger Nairobi campus, Claire's passion for photography drew her to a smaller, more remote one. She envisioned building a portfolio of Kenya's most iconic wildlife and sweeping panoramas—images that she hoped would bring her closer to her dream of becoming a professional photographer.

But deep down, Claire knew there was more to this trip than cultural immersion or chasing her photographic dreams. It was mostly an escape.

Since her brother's death, grief had become a shadow she couldn't outrun—heavy and ever-present. At home, all she found were pitying stares, her parents' overbearing love, and a hollow ache that refused to fade. Kenya felt like the only place far enough away.

Her father's words still echoed in her memory. "You're running away, Claire. Leaving won't fix anything."

"I'm not running away," she had insisted, her voice rising defensively. "I just...I need space, Dad. I can't breathe here anymore."

"And you think going halfway across the world will help?" His voice had cracked, his frustration giving way to pain. "How much space do you need?"

She had recognized the truth in his words, even then. But this trip was a chance to reclaim the part of herself untouched by sorrow, a chance to begin again.

"Zebras!" A classmate's excited shout jerked her back to the present.

The bus skidded to a halt, kicking up a thick cloud of dust. Claire peered through the dirty window and spotted them—a small herd, grazing just yards away. Their black-and-white stripes shimmered in the afternoon heat, surreal against the golden savanna.

She quickly snatched up her cell phone. Around her, cameras erupted like celebratory fireworks, shutters clicking in rapid succession.

She framed the perfect shot, finger poised over the screen—

Then, it flickered. A second later…black.

Battery dead.

Great.

Claire slumped back into her seat, her useless phone still clutched tightly in her hand. The bus lurched forward, the engine complaining as it picked up speed, leaving the zebras, and her missed opportunity, behind.

When they finally arrived at the campus gate, she let out a weary sigh of relief. A sliver of anticipation cut through her fatigue as she remembered the program brochure.

The campus was described as a scenic "oasis for learning," complete with sturdy and inviting dormitories, classrooms bathed in golden sunlight, and picturesque grounds bordered by colorful flowers.

But as the bus rumbled through the gate and rolled to a stop in the heart of the compound, Claire's stomach bottomed out.

Her "dream come true" was nothing more than a mirage, vanishing before her eyes.

Chapter 2

Pamoja Global School

Claire pressed a hand against the window, her breath fogging the glass as she took in the scene before her.

The "inviting" dorms were little more than crumbling shells, their paint peeling in ragged strips to reveal weathered concrete beneath. The windows were gaping holes, while thick strips of fabric, nailed haphazardly into place, served as makeshift doors.

The classrooms were flimsy structures that lacked walls entirely. Hard wooden benches were fastened to concrete slabs beneath roofs patched together with rusted, corrugated metal.

Claire's shoulders slumped, and a bitter laugh escaped her. "This is *unbelievable*," she muttered.

Beside her, the young man grinned, his camera clicking nonstop. "You're right! It *is* unbelievable!"

Claire shot him a look, baffled by his enthusiasm. *What does he see in this rundown campus that's worth that many pictures?* she wondered bitterly.

As she stepped off the bus, a sudden burst of color flashed before her. A woman approached the group draped in an azure skirt that shimmered like the summer sky. Her wrists were adorned with vibrant beaded jewelry in a dazzling array of colors.

"Welcome to Pamoja Global School!" she boomed, her voice rich with warmth and energy. "Pamoja means *together* in

Swahili which is a perfect reflection of our campus mission: collaboration for mutual growth." She beamed. "I'm Naomi, your house mother."

With a welcoming gesture, Naomi beckoned the students to follow her toward the dormitories. Excited chatter erupted—names exchanged, first impressions made, voices buzzing with nervous energy.

But Claire trailed behind them, her steps slower, her mood heavier. She was quite aware that, unlike her peers, she had nothing to unpack.

When they reached the girl's dormitory, she braced herself for another round of disappointment. But as she walked inside, she let out a surprised gasp.

Sunlight streamed through the open windows, dancing across a freshly mopped floor that gleamed like polished glass. Twelve single beds lined the walls, each topped with clean linens and draped with airy white mosquito nets that swayed gently in the breeze. Beside each bed sat a small desk and dresser, offering a practical touch of comfort.

The room was simple, but the cheery interior was unexpectedly inviting. It sparked a small glint of hope in her, like a wildflower stubbornly pushing its way through cracked pavement.

She chose a bed tucked away in the corner, its quiet seclusion offering a tenuous promise of peace. Before long, a chorus of questions filled the air.

"Are there any screens for the windows?" a petite girl asked Naomi.

"No, child," the woman replied. "You will appreciate any breeze that comes through those openings, especially during the hot evenings."

"But what about animals? Won't they climb in through the windows?" another girl inquired nervously.

Naomi chuckled, a rich sound that filled the room. "The fences should stop our larger animals from entering the compound, but monkeys are clever little things," she said with a grin. "Every so often, one manages to sneak into the dorms looking for a midnight snack. So, keep your food secure."

Then as she turned to leave, she added, "Meet me in the dining room in one hour. We have a welcome dinner planned for you tonight!"

Claire hurried over to her before she reached the door. "Excuse me, Naomi? The airline lost my luggage. Is there any place where I can buy some clothing and essentials?"

Naomi's expression softened. "I'm sorry, dear. There aren't any shops nearby, but maybe the other girls can lend you something." With that, Naomi vanished, leaving Claire feeling stranded and disappointed.

"Perfect," Claire muttered as she returned to her bed, picturing herself wearing the same clothes for the next few weeks.

"Need something to borrow?" a voice asked.

Claire spun around to find a girl standing beside the adjacent bed. She had kind brown eyes and a cascade of wavy, beach-blonde hair that fell to her shoulders.

"Hi, I'm Rachel," she introduced herself, her tone as warm as her smile.

Claire was hesitant. "I don't want to impose."

Rachel waved her off. "Nonsense! I totally overpacked anyway. Here," she said, heaving her suitcase onto Claire's bed and popping it open. "Take whatever you need."

With a nod, Claire grabbed a T-shirt and black athletic pants. The simple gesture warmed her in a way she hadn't anticipated.

"Thank you, Rachel," Claire responded, with genuine gratitude in her voice. "This means a lot, especially after the day I've had. I'm Claire, by the way."

"Nice to meet you," Rachel beamed. "And seriously, don't mention it. What are roommates for?"

As Claire placed the borrowed clothes in her dresser, her gaze fell on something nestled among Rachel's belongings—a leather-bound Bible.

A heavy ache spread through her chest, the kind that made breathing feel like a chore. She could almost feel the familiar weight of her own Bible, the worn cover pressed into her trembling hands as she knelt beside her brother's hospital bed.

The memory surged back—her whispered, desperate pleas to God to heal the cancer ravaging his fragile body. Only silence had answered.

His death had shattered her faith, leaving an empty void where belief once lived.

Her eyes stung, blurring the edges of her vision. The walls pressed in, the air too thick to breathe.

She pushed to her feet and stepped outside. Maybe a walk under the open sky would clear her head.

Above, the evening sky blazed with vivid hues of orange and crimson as the first stars emerged like watchful sentinels against the creeping twilight. A soft breeze swept through, carrying the sweet fragrance of unfamiliar flowers, while distant birdsong reached her ears like a faint melody.

Claire drew in a slow, measured breath. For the briefest moment, a glimmer of optimism pierced through her gloom.

Maybe this semester in Kenya is just what I need—the chance to move on and rebuild my life.

But as quickly as hope flickered to life, sorrow snuffed it out. The thought of forging a future without her brother felt like a betrayal, a silent concession that he was truly gone.

Her steps slowed, then stopped entirely. Claire glanced around, an unfamiliar path stretching before her. She was lost—not just in Kenya, but in the vast, uncharted wilderness of her own grief.

She had traveled halfway across the world in search of an escape, longing to piece together the shattered remnants of her life.

But standing here, thousands of miles from home, she felt more trapped than ever.

Will I ever know peace again? The question loomed over her

like a dark cloud.
> *Or am I destined to carry this pain forever?*

Chapter 3

Circle of Friends

Claire woke early the next morning, determined to put the previous day's misery behind her and start fresh. Though the setbacks had left her battered and drained, she refused to let them define her semester on campus.

She dressed quickly, tying her long black hair into a tight ponytail and lacing up her sneakers. As she stood up, her roommate stirred in the bed beside her.

"You're up early," Rachel mumbled groggily. Her messy blonde hair was a halo of chaos.

Claire tucked her earbuds into her pocket. "Morning run."

Rachel groaned. "Gotcha. Hey, if you see coffee anywhere on campus, could you bring me a cup? I'd die for some right about now."

"I'll see what I can do," she replied with a smile, before stepping outside.

Running had always been her sanctuary—a way to quiet her thoughts and renew her energy. Today, it felt like the perfect way to reset. With any luck, she wouldn't get lost this time.

As she jogged through the campus, the cool air filled her lungs, invigorating her with each stride. Just ahead, a sudden flash of color caught her eye. A group of Maasai women moved gracefully along the path, their vibrant jewelry standing out against the muted, earthy tones of the landscape.

Stepping aside to let them pass, she felt a thrill. She'd

spent hours researching the Maasai tribe before her trip, learning about their traditions and colorful jewelry, but nothing compared to seeing them up close.

Their voices, rich and rhythmic, wove together like a melody in a language she couldn't understand. Yet, there was a warmth in their easy interactions, a natural grace in the way they moved together. As they disappeared down the path, a sudden pang of loneliness caught her off guard.

Maybe that's what I need. A community of my own.

Spending the semester alone wasn't an option. Not again. Solitude had consumed her since her brother's death, and if she wanted a fresh start, she had to push herself and try to connect with her classmates.

To her relief, making friends turned out to be easier than she had anticipated. Her roommate, Rachel, was a natural starting point. With her quintessential California-girl charm, sunny disposition, and outgoing personality, Rachel was the perfect counterbalance to Claire's quieter, more reserved nature. Before long, a genuine friendship began to blossom between them.

Claire's circle of friends grew even wider when she met a fellow student named Daniel during one of her morning runs. She had just rounded a corner when a voice called out behind her.

"Hey! Mind if I join you?"

She glanced over her shoulder to see a short, athletic guy with a friendly face jogging to catch up.

"Sure," she replied, adjusting her pace slightly.

"I'm Daniel," he said, falling into step beside her. "I see you out here every morning. Figured it was about time I introduced myself. You know, before it gets weird."

She laughed. "I'm Claire."

"Hey. So, what's your excuse for torturing yourself with early-morning runs? Fitness fanatic? Or just trying to run away from all your responsibilities?"

She smirked, catching the teasing in his tone. "A little bit of both, I guess. Running clears my head, and it's the only time I don't feel guilty for ignoring my homework."

"Smart," Daniel remarked, nodding approvingly. "Me? I run for the pancakes. Gotta make room for all the carbs, you know?"

"Solid strategy," she said with a grin.

Their easy banter continued as they jogged along, and by the time they looped back toward the dorms, Claire felt like she'd found a kindred spirit.

It wasn't long before she introduced him to Rachel and the three became inseparable, their bond solidified through shared laughter and long conversations. For the first time since her arrival, she experienced a genuine sense of belonging as she eased into the rhythm of campus life.

Within a few weeks, another figure on campus caught her attention—Professor Miller. Young, charismatic, and brimming with energy, he brought Anthropology to life, weaving tales of ancient cultures and lost civilizations with the flair of a storyteller. To his students, he was a modern-day Indiana Jones, complete with an infectious enthusiasm that made even the driest topics fascinating.

Yet, it wasn't just his teaching style that drew Claire in.

Whenever she looked up, she'd catch him watching her—not in a passing glance, but with deliberate focus. The instant their eyes met, he'd snap his gaze away—too quickly.

Was it a simple concern for her academics? Or something else?

Determined to solve the mystery, Claire lingered after class one afternoon, pretending to review her notes. As the last students filtered out, she made her way to his desk.

"Professor Miller?"

He looked up, his warm, intelligent eyes meeting hers. "Yes? How can I help you?"

Claire held up her notebook. "I had a question about the homework. The ethnographic case study. How detailed should our analysis be?"

He leaned back slightly, considering. "Good question. I want depth, yes, but don't get so lost in the details that you miss the bigger picture. Focus on the key themes."

She scribbled down his response. No closer to an answer, she sighed quietly and turned to leave.

"Miss Thompson." The professor's voice stopped her.

She glanced back. His tone had shifted—softer now, more personal.

"I'm sorry to hear about your missing luggage. It must be hard being so far from home without your things."

"How...how could you possibly know that?" she stammered.

He smiled, a hint of mischief dancing in his blue eyes. "Well, I'm quite observant," he admitted. "I've noticed you've been alternating between two outfits for weeks. One yours, and the other borrowed, I'm guessing." Professor Miller leaned forward slightly, his voice smooth. "You see, I make it my business to know *everything* that happens on this campus."

Heat rushed to her cheeks as the mystery unraveled in an instant. He wasn't personally interested in her at all, he just had a sharp eye for details. She scolded herself for letting herself get carried away.

"Well, I hope your luggage shows up soon," he continued. "It must be exhausting keeping up the rotation."

"It is," she admitted, smiling despite her lingering embarrassment. Then she added, "To be honest, though, it's not the clothes I miss the most. My new Sony camera was in that luggage. I came here hoping to photograph wildlife and landscapes, but until it's found, I'll have to settle for imagining the shots."

A smile spread across his face. "Photography? That's wonderful! I am also passionate about shooting the wildlife here. Especially the Big Five."

"The Big Five?"

He nodded. "Yes. Kenya's most celebrated animals—the lion, leopard, buffalo, elephant, and black rhino." Then he hesitated briefly before adding, "Once your camera arrives, I'd be happy to recommend a few spots to find them."

"That would be amazing!" she gushed. "I'd love any tips you have."

"There's an animal reserve not far from here called Maasai Mara. It's a photographer's paradise. I know the area well." He met her gaze, his voice almost casual. "If you'd like a guide, I could take you there on one of my days off. Once your camera shows up, of course."

Her eyes widened. "Really?"

"Absolutely," he said with a warm smile.

As Claire stepped outside the classroom, excitement surged through her.

She wasn't sure if it was the thrill of photographing Kenya's iconic wildlife or the possibility that Professor Miller's glances might not be her overactive imagination after all.

Chapter 4

Lost & Found

The next afternoon, her suitcase arrived like the prodigal son, beaten up but back home. Claire knelt beside it, her fingers tracing the dents and scratches, each one a reminder of its chaotic journey through the bowels of the airline's baggage system.

Claire unlatched the case, the familiar scent of home rising from its depths, wrapping around her like a warm embrace.

But only one item truly mattered.

Her fingers dug past the neatly folded clothes, seeking the cool, smooth surface of her camera—the heart of her Kenyan adventure. She lifted it gingerly and turned it over in her hands, examining it for any sign of trauma.

Please be okay. Please be okay.

Her fingers hovered over the power button. She pressed it, and for a second, nothing happened.

Then, the screen flickered to life. Claire exhaled a breath she hadn't realized she was holding. No cracks. No error messages. No shattered lens.

Miraculously, it was perfect!

"Guess what!" Claire exclaimed over dinner with Rachel and Daniel. "My wayward luggage has finally arrived! And even better, my camera survived the journey intact!"

She was beaming as she plopped down next to Daniel, her

relief making her feel lighter.

"When did you first get into photography?" he asked, leaning back in his chair as he popped a fry into his mouth.

Claire's expression brightened. "It was because of my brother, Tyler. One Christmas, he got this fancy camera, and suddenly, he was everywhere, snapping photos of what seemed like the most random things. Cracks in the sidewalks, reflections in the windows...stuff I thought was boring. But then he showed me the photos. It was like he made the ordinary look...magical."

"So, he got you into it?" Daniel asked, leaning forward, clearly interested.

"Yeah. A few months later, I saved up for my own camera. But instead of city shots, I was more into wildlife and nature. It just felt...right. I've been hooked ever since." Her voice softened, her gaze drifting as if she were seeing the world through her lens. "I dream about becoming a professional photographer one day. Traveling the world...capturing it all."

"That's amazing. Is that why you decided to study in Africa?" Daniel asked.

Her smile faltered slightly. "It was...one of the reasons," she stated, her tone quieter now.

Daniel, oblivious to the subtle change in her mood, pressed on. "Tyler must be proud that you're chasing your dream. Is he older or younger?"

The hum of the dining hall receded like someone had turned down the volume. Claire's fingers tightened on her fork. She hesitated, the words catching in her throat.

"He is... I mean, he was..." Her voice cracked. She tried to control herself, but it was too late.

The dam broke.

"Daniel, will you just...SHUT UP about my brother?"

The words came out louder than she intended, echoing across the dining room. A few heads turned toward their table.

Daniel's face paled. "Oh—uh, I'm...I'm so sorry. I didn't mean to—"

Claire looked down as tears threatened to spill. She hadn't

meant to snap, hadn't meant for her grief to burst out in the middle of dinner like this.

After a moment, she exhaled slowly, forcing herself to meet his eyes. Her voice was barely above a whisper.

"No, it's me. *I'm* sorry. I shouldn't have...yelled like that. It's just...I don't like talking about him."

Daniel's expression softened. "Hey, it's okay."

Rachel, who had been silent until now, reached across the table and placed a gentle hand on Claire's arm. The touch was simple but grounding—a wordless reassurance that she had found friends who cared about her...and she wasn't alone.

Daniel quickly shifted the conversation to homework, sports—anything else. Grateful for the change of subject, Claire let herself breathe again, hoping she hadn't ruined their budding friendship.

After dinner, Naomi gathered the students for a brief meeting. Standing at the front of the dining hall with a warm yet authoritative presence, she clapped her hands together. The chatter in the room gradually died down.

"I hope these first few weeks have helped you settle in," she began. "As you know, our school values collaboration and mutual growth. Part of that philosophy includes contributing to the daily life of our campus."

A few students exchanged wary glances, sensing where this was going.

"Which is why," Naomi continued with a knowing smile, "each of you will be assigned a campus job."

A collective groan rippled through the group.

As Naomi read through the list—"Britney...office, Steven...maintenance, Rosie...cleaning"—the reactions varied from mild grumbling to resigned nods.

Claire straightened in her seat, her anticipation growing as the list neared her name. She had noticed a few Maasai women working in the kitchen and silently hoped for the chance to join them.

"Claire Thompson?" Naomi called out.

"Here," she called out, bracing herself.

"Kitchen duty."

Of all the assignments, this felt like a gift—an opportunity to work alongside the women and experience their culture up close. After the disaster of dinner, it was a small but welcome piece of good news.

Feeling a little better after the meeting, she decided to stop by Professor Miller's office. She couldn't wait to tell him that her camera had finally arrived.

When she shared the news, he exclaimed, "That's fantastic, Miss Thompson." He leaned back slightly, considering something. "The nature reserve is open from sunrise to sunset. If you're still interested, I'm available next Saturday."

Her eyes lit up, unable to hide her excitement. "Oh, absolutely!" Then, after a brief hesitation, she offered, "And, um…you can just call me Claire, if that's okay."

"All right, Claire," he replied, his voice warm. "I'll reserve the school's Jeep for next Saturday. It's got a sunroof, perfect for viewing animals. Oh, and when it's just us, Peter will do."

Surprised by the informality, a small flush warmed her cheeks. "Okay…Peter," she replied quietly, tucking a loose strand of hair behind her ear.

As she strolled back to her dorm, her mind danced with images of Africa's wildlife—lions basking in the sunshine, hippos wading through the river, giraffes silhouetted against the vast savanna. In just one week, her photographic adventure would begin.

Inside the dorm, the room pulsed with energy as voices overlapped and laughter crackled like electricity. It took her a second to catch on. The whitewater rafting trip on the Tana River was the next day.

Between the day's chaos and her plans with Professor Miller, the field trip had completely slipped her mind. Quickly shifting gears, she rummaged through her belongings, quickly tossing items into her backpack.

Rachel flopped down on Claire's bed, grinning. "There you

are! Aren't you excited? This is going to be epic! There are five rapids, a waterfall, and tons of wildlife!"

Claire offered a small smile, trying to match Rachel's energy.

Rachel's brow lifted. "You *are* looking forward to it, right?"

"Yeah, it sounds amazing. It's just...I guess I'm a little distracted. I found out I'm going to an animal reserve next week to photograph wildlife with...um, Professor Miller."

Rachel sat up straight, her grin turning mischievous. "Professor Miller? Ohhh, I see. No wonder you're a *little* distracted."

Claire burst out laughing, shaking her head. "It's not like that. He's just going to be my guide!"

They dissolved into giggles and soon were caught up in an animated conversation—about the rafting trip, the wildlife they couldn't wait to see, and, of course, the undeniably charming professor.

They talked late into the night until exhaustion finally caught up with them.

As Claire climbed into bed, vivid scenes of African wildlife and sweeping landscapes drifted through her mind. Yet, as sleep gently claimed her, it wasn't lions or elephants that tarried in her thoughts.

It was a pair of mesmerizing blue eyes.

Chapter 5

Rafting Adventure

Twenty-five students gathered around the school bus as the first light of dawn stretched across the Pamoja Global School, casting a golden glow over the eager group. Anticipation crackled in the cool morning air as they waited for their adventure.

At the bus entrance, Naomi moved swiftly through the line, handing each student a piece of flatbread, a banana, and a bottle of water—provisions for the journey ahead. Yawns punctuated their conversations as they shook off the remnants of sleep.

Claire claimed seats near the front of the bus with Rachel and Daniel, determined to avoid the bone-rattling chaos of the back row. The memory of her first day's whiplash-inducing ride was still fresh in her mind, and she had no intention of repeating it.

As the bus came to life and rolled forward, most of the students gazed sleepily out the window, watching the shifting landscape.

But Rachel, buzzing with energy, had other ideas.

"Okay, listen up!" she declared, her voice brimming with confidence. "Class 2 and 3 rapids are pretty easy to handle. The key is keeping your hands on the paddle's T-grip. One hand has to stay on it at all times, or you'll risk smacking the rest of us with your paddle. And trust me, no one wants that."

She paused, leaning forward to demonstrate the perfectly executed stroke. Straightening with a triumphant smile, she asked, "Got it?"

Daniel flashed her a teasing grin. "Hold on, Rach. Are you saying if I don't master this *right now*, I'm destined to give someone a black eye? Because honestly, there's no way Claire and I are going to remember all that."

Rachel sighed dramatically, throwing her hands into the air. "But I haven't even told you about the most important part!" she exclaimed, a hint of exasperation in her voice. "Toward the end of the course, we'll encounter the class five rapids called the Captain's Folly, Can of Worms, and Sphincter Flexor, and you'll need the sweep stroke for those—"

"W-wait, what?" Daniel interrupted, his words tripping over his laughter. "Someone actually named a rapid the *Can of Worms*?"

Claire, already chuckling, managed to ask, "Rachel, how do you even know that?"

"It's in the brochure," Rachel admitted, half exasperated, half amused. "I thought you'd appreciate a little heads-up, but clearly, I overestimated your maturity level."

Daniel raised his hands in defense, a playful smirk spread across his face. "Hey, that's on you. How is anyone supposed to take something called *Sphincter Flexor* seriously?"

"You walked right into that one," Claire chimed in.

Rachel finally gave in, letting out a playful sigh as a wide smile replaced her earlier frustration. "Fine. Laugh it up," she said, her tone light and playful now. "But don't come crying to me when you're hurtling through the Can of Worms, clinging for dear life, and wishing you'd practiced that sweep stroke!"

Her teasing reignited Daniel and Claire's laughter, their voices ringing through the bus. Rachel tried to keep a straight face but couldn't hold out for long, eventually joining in, shaking her head at the absurdity of it all.

When the bus rumbled to a stop at Sagana Rapids Camp, the students piled out, eager to stretch their legs after the long ride. Then they headed to the locker rooms to change into wetsuits before gathering for a safety briefing.

The camp staff, a charismatic group of tanned and energetic individuals, passed around fresh coffee before diving into the safety procedures.

Claire watched their demonstrations of hand signals and paddle strokes, trying to commit each motion to memory. But she knew if she faltered, Rachel would know what to do.

Then, the lead instructor stepped forward. An Australian man with a booming voice who commanded the group's full attention.

"Alrighty, mates! Listen up! This river here is teeming with life, and I don't just mean fish."

Claire's stomach gave a nervous flip. *This doesn't sound reassuring.*

"Sometimes, crocodiles like to sun themselves along the riverbanks, so the key is to keep your distance. Remember this saying: 'See a croc, don't gawk. Paddle away, or you'll rue the day!'"

The man chuckled at his own joke. The students, however, exchanged uncertain glances. But before anyone could question his advice, he clapped his hands together, launching into his next point.

"Now, as for snakes, they sometimes drop into your raft from the branches overhead."

As a sharp inhale spread through the group, Claire's pulse kicked up a notch. *Did I hear that right?*

"Just remember, don't panic or flail around. Just grab it, and toss it back into the river."

Jittery giggles rippled through the crowd, as if they were waiting for confirmation that this was a joke. Claire, however, wasn't sure whether to laugh or rethink her life choices.

The instructor grinned but didn't clarify. "Alright, let's get crackin'!"

Before she had time to dwell on it, the students rushed toward the rafts, a mix of excitement and pure adrenaline driving them forward.

Claire, Rachel, and Daniel climbed into a bright blue raft, third in a line of six, bobbing impatiently among the flotilla. Up ahead, the first raft lurched forward, its passengers whooping as they were swallowed by the roaring current.

At last, it was their turn!

With a shove from the bank, the raft launched into the choppy current. Claire clutched the raft's edge, her knuckles white as icy water splashed against her legs. The river's deep rumble grew into a deafening roar as they picked up speed, hurtling toward the first rapid.

"Lean to the right! Now left! Paddle hard! Use the sweep stroke! Avoid that rock!"

The camp oarsman barked commands in rapid succession, his voice rising over the rush of water. Claire shot an anxious glance at Rachel, but her face radiated focused determination.

Mirroring her movements, Claire dug her paddle into the water. With a final, powerful surge, they broke through the first rapid, emerging on the other side with triumphant shouts.

Up ahead, the telltale white crests of the next rapid churned violently, far more intense than the last. Jagged rocks, some the size of small cars, jutted ominously from the water's surface.

"Is this the Can of Worms?" Claire tried to shout, but her voice was drowned out by the deafening roar of the water.

Claire looked over at Rachel again, but her calm confidence helped to steady her nerves. Together, they braved the turbulent currents, maneuvering between the rocks. A final swell sent them soaring over the last drop before they crashed into smooth water on the other side—soaked but victorious.

The river opened into a tranquil pool, a welcome contrast to the adrenaline-filled adventure they had just passed through. Beside it, a breathtaking waterfall cascaded down a rocky cliff, sending shimmering mist into the air.

The other rafts had already stopped, their passengers

splashing happily in the warm water or standing beneath the thundering waterfall.

The three friends eagerly joined the other students, diving into the refreshing water. It was a welcome respite, a chance to appreciate the waterfall's beauty and the natural wonders of their surroundings.

After a swim, Claire and her friends settled on the riverbank, letting the sun warm their skin as they shared their thoughts on the trip.

"That last rapid was so much scarier than the first one," Claire confessed.

"No kidding," Daniel agreed. "But Rachel was so calm, and that helped me keep it together."

Rachel shrugged, smiling confidently. "Honestly, it wasn't that bad. Pretty tame, really."

Daniel smirked, throwing Claire a knowing glance. "Right. Tame. Meanwhile, I thought we were all about to go over the side."

Rachel laughed. "You guys did awesome, especially for your first time! But I knew we'd be fine."

"Oh yeah?" Claire asked. "And what made you so sure?"

"Because I asked God to watch over us," she stated matter-of-factly.

"You really think that's why we made it through?" Claire asked.

Rachel tilted her head, studying her. "Sure, I do. Why not?"

Claire paused, her voice quieter now. "Because it's…hard to believe there's a God out there who actually cares about what happens to us."

"What makes you feel that way?" Rachel asked gently.

Claire's words caught in her throat. A year ago, prayer had been second nature, as easy as breathing. But now, bitterness filled the space where faith once dwelt.

"I used to pray," she admitted. "But then…"

Claire paused. *Can I trust Rachel and Daniel with this? Will they understand my grief?*

But then looked at them—really taking them in. There was no pressure, no judgment. Just two people who cared, patiently waiting for her to let them in.

For the first time in a long while, she found the courage to share her loss.

"Then my brother, Tyler, was diagnosed with colon cancer," she murmured. "By the time they found it, it was already stage four. He…he never even had a chance."

Daniel's face fell. "The brother I asked you about at dinner last night? I'm so sorry. I had no idea."

"You couldn't have known." she managed an apologetic smile before continuing. "I begged God to heal him, but my brother died anyway. He was only nineteen. Since that day, I decided I couldn't follow a God who abandoned me when I needed Him the most."

She lowered her head, her shoulders trembling under the burden of her sorrow. Without a word, Rachel and Daniel leaned in, wrapping her in a gentle embrace.

They didn't try to speak. There was no need. Their reassuring presence, warm and steady, offered a comfort far deeper than words ever could.

A sharp whistle pierced the air, signaling the end of the break. Claire gave her friends a shaky smile, grateful for their understanding. Together, the three returned to their raft and tackled the remaining rapids with renewed determination.

At the end of their adventure, the students returned to camp, drenched but exhilarated. They quickly changed into dry clothes before eating their packed lunches.

Later, on the bus ride home, the gentle hum of the engine lulled most of their classmates to sleep. But Claire, Daniel, and Rachel stayed awake, chatting quietly. With each shared story or burst of laughter, an invisible bridge stretched between them—one that promised a friendship lasting far beyond their time in Kenya.

As the bus entered the campus gates, Rachel leaned over and whispered to Claire, "If you ever want to talk about God, whether you believe He cares or not, just reach out to me. No pressure. I'm here to listen, no matter what you believe."

Claire responded with a small, grateful nod, moved by her friend's compassion.

Walking back to the dorm, a faint ray of optimism took root in Claire's heart. But it wasn't the rafting adventure that lifted her spirits—it was the simple act of opening up to Rachel and Daniel. Their kindness and acceptance had begun to chip away at the grief she had carried for so long.

For the first time in ages, she didn't feel like she was merely surviving. She was genuinely looking forward to the days ahead.

And in just one week, her next adventure would begin—her excursion with Professor Miller. Though she couldn't fully explain it, something told her his journey would be unlike any other.

And when it was over, nothing would be the same.

Chapter 6

Elephant Attack

As the first streaks of dawn painted the sky in fiery hues, Claire gripped the side of the borrowed Jeep, her heart pounding with excitement. Beside her, Peter navigated the dirt road with ease, the vehicle rattling over the uneven terrain. A thick cloud of red dust billowed behind them, momentarily eclipsing the world in their wake.

The week leading up to the Maasai Mara excursion had crawled by, each day stretching longer than the last. Claire's mind buzzed with expectancy, her thoughts constantly drifting to the endless grassy plains and the elusive wildlife that roamed them.

Finally, Saturday arrived.

Peter, ever the seasoned traveler, lounged comfortably in the driver's seat, a bright grin beneath the brim of his weathered hat.

"Beautiful morning, isn't it?" he remarked, his tone light, like they were on a casual Sunday drive rather than bouncing down a remote dirt track.

Before she could respond, the road suddenly vanished.

The Jeep lurched forward, its tires plunging into an unexpected rush of river water. A startled gasp caught in Claire's throat as the current surged around them, lapping at the wheels. Her fingers clamped around the overhead handle, her grip tightening with every inch the car sank deeper.

"Is this, um, safe?" she asked, her voice strained.

Peter only chuckled, completely unfazed. "Absolutely!"

She wasn't convinced. The water churned higher, tugging at the vehicle like it wanted to swallow them whole.

"Are you sure?" she pressed. "Because it looks like we're sinking."

He merely gestured toward the hood. "Relax. This baby's got a snorkel."

"I'm sorry—a what?"

"It keeps the engine from sucking in water," he replied, nonchalantly.

Despite Peter's reassurances, Claire refused to breathe until the tires climbed onto solid ground on the far bank. Only then did she release a long exhale, her fingers sore from gripping the handle.

"See?" He shot her a sideways glance. "That wasn't so bad."

Claire gave him an exasperated look. "Easy for you to say. I don't even know what a snorkel is!"

Peter laughed, his blue eyes twinkling with amusement.

It took a few minutes for her nerves to settle, but soon, she found herself drawn back to the beauty around her.

As they approached the reserve's entrance, Claire noticed a small Maasai village nestled beside the roadside. The mud huts, thatched roofs, and colorfully dressed inhabitants painted a picturesque scene. Wisps of smoke curled from the dwellings, while Maasai men in red garments watched over grazing goats with quiet dignity.

"Can we stop by this village after the reserve?" she asked eagerly. "I'd love to take some pictures of it."

"We can ask. But the Maasai don't always allow photography."

A few minutes later, they passed through the grand green gate of the Maasai Mara reserve. Beyond it, the landscape unfolded like a masterpiece: golden grasses rippling in waves beneath an endless blue sky, the horizon punctuated by clusters of acacia trees.

"Wow," she murmured, gripping her camera firmly. "It's like stepping into another world. Everything feels so...endless."

He glanced over from the driver's seat. "This place has a way of reminding you how small you are, but in the best possible way."

The first hour was spent navigating winding dirt paths that carved through the vast reserve. The sheer expanse of the area was staggering, making it difficult to spot wildlife among the thousands of acres of land. But they pressed on undeterred, carefully scanning the plains.

All of a sudden, Peter exclaimed, "There!" pointing to the west.

Claire's heart soared. A herd of elephants!

He eased the Jeep to a stop at a respectful distance, giving them the perfect vantage to watch the majestic procession.

The elephants moved with grace, their wrinkled gray bodies swaying in unison as they crossed the road. Their footsteps rumbled beneath them, the vibrations pulsing through the vehicle.

Eager for a better view, Claire scrambled into the backseat and popped her head out of the sunroof.

The herd moved in perfect harmony, their uniform rhythm unbroken until each one disappeared into a sea of golden grass on the far side of the road. The final elephant brought up the rear with her small calf trotting close by her side.

Peter eased the car forward, following the pair cautiously. In the backseat, Claire began to capture the scene, each shutter click preserving a memory of this incredible encounter. As she zoomed in, the mother elephant and her calf were so close, it felt as though she could almost touch them.

"I think we better go," Peter called back. "It's not safe being this far from the main road."

"Just one more," she pleaded, aiming her camera again.

As if in response, the massive creature abruptly stopped, turned, and fixed a piercing gaze directly at her.

Claire braced her hands and pressed the shutter. In that

moment, she knew she had taken a photo of something truly unforgettable.

Suddenly, an earth-shattering trumpet tore through the air, the elephant's long ears flaring like battle flags. Claire gasped as the giant creature charged toward the Jeep with alarming speed.

Peter reacted instantly, slamming the vehicle into reverse and tearing backward through the tall grass. She cried out, thrown off balance, scrambling for anything to hold onto.

Despite the swirling dust and the icy grip of fear, Claire's gaze was irresistibly drawn back to the elephant. The majestic creature was gone, replaced by a fierce, raging force.

"Faster! Peter, drive faster!" she shrieked.

The ground quaked beneath them as the animal closed the distance. Peter yanked the wheel, executing a sharp swerve to straighten their course. Claire was thrown sideways, crashing down to the seat before tumbling to the floor.

The elephant finally caught up with them, slamming into the back of the Jeep with a bone-rattling crash. Claire was flung again—her head smashing into the side door.

"Aaaaah!" Her scream tore through the chaos. Stars exploded in her vision as a searing pain shot down her neck.

She braced herself, her body tensing in anticipation of another strike. But it never came.

Blinking through the haze of disorientation, her eyes darted around, desperately searching for any sign of the massive animal. But the creature had disappeared.

Is it over?

Without missing a beat, Peter slammed his foot on the gas, sending the Jeep hurtling toward the main road. The vehicle skidded to a halt at the roadside, its battered frame groaning under the strain.

Peter jumped out and yanked open the back door. "Claire! Are you alright?"

Still wobbly, she touched the side of her head. "I…I think so. I hit my head, but I don't think it's too bad."

He reached out, his fingers gently pulling back her hair to examine the wound. Finding a small red lump, he released a sigh.

"Just a bump. Thank goodness. But maybe we should get you checked out anyway, just to be safe."

"No!" she shook her head, sitting up a little straighter. "I want to keep going. I just need some ice."

He considered it for a moment, then nodded. "Okay. There's a lodge about ten miles away. Let's stop there."

Claire scrambled back into her seat as Peter started the engine and steered the battered vehicle toward the resort. Her once-in-a-lifetime photo now seemed like a distant dream, overshadowed by the throbbing pain in her head.

Minutes of silence passed before she spoke. "I can't believe how fast that elephant turned us," she murmured. "One second, she's staring at me so calmly, and the next, she's charging—like she was out for blood!"

"We were in her territory, acting unpredictably around her calf," he explained. "Elephants are wild animals, Claire. They'll never be calm or docile. They're immensely powerful, and when they feel threatened, they've been known to ram or flip cars. Honestly, we got off lucky."

"Lucky?" she shot back as she rubbed her temples. "You call that lucky? I thought we were going to die!"

Peter's expression grew dark. "I had a close call myself a few years ago. I got overconfident, got too close to an elephant, and…well, let's just say I learned the hard way to respect their territory." He held up his arm, revealing a faint but unmistakable scar etched across his skin.

Tiny goosebumps prickled her arms. "I guess we *were* lucky," she admitted softly.

Peter's frown melted into one of his dazzling smiles. "Absolutely. Now, let's get you to that lodge. You're going to love it! It's quite stunning inside, and they'll make sure you're well taken care of."

She nodded absently, her gaze drifting to the window as

the landscape rushed past in a blur of golden grass and dust. Her mind replayed the horrifying event—the deafening thunder that shook the ground and the overwhelming force of the creature's wrath.

It left her feeling small, vulnerable...and utterly outmatched.

The boundary between observing nature and intruding upon it had never felt so thin. And in that moment, she made a silent vow.

She would never place herself at the mercy of the untamed wild again.

Chapter 7

Life & Death on the Savanna

Twenty minutes later, the lodge emerged on the horizon, an elegant fortress of mahogany, its towering frame a stark contrast to the wilderness they had just escaped.

Yet, despite its imposing structure, lush greenery framed its entrance, vibrant flowers burst in brilliant reds and gold, and exotic foliage lined the pathways, creating a harmonious blend with the reserve's natural beauty—as if it had been there forever.

It was beautiful. Luxurious. Safe.

"Wow," Claire murmured as she scanned the enormous structure.

A few minutes later, Peter pushed open the heavy wooden doors, and they stepped into a sanctuary of tranquility.

Golden sunlight streamed through floor-to-ceiling windows, casting a warm glow over the plush sofas and deep armchairs that invited weary travelers to sink into their comfort. Along the walls, vibrant African artwork whispered tales of the land and its people.

Peter flagged down a passing attendant. "Ice, aspirin, and a cup of chai tea, please."

He then led Claire to a cozy corner of the lobby, where she sank gratefully into a chair layered with soft cushions.

Moments later, the attendant returned with the order. The ice's cool touch felt heavenly against the throbbing pain in her temple, and the spiced chai tea spread warmth through her like a soothing balm.

For the first time since the encounter, she exhaled fully, letting the lodge's serene atmosphere melt away the stiffness that still clung to her muscles.

From her seat, she quietly observed the rhythm of the lobby, the subtle hum of wealth and adventure weaving around her. Well-dressed tourists conversed excitedly over their itineraries, their dreams of an African safari about to unfold. Guides, porters, and hotel staff moved seamlessly through the space, anticipating their every need.

"This place is incredible," she noted, taking in the elegance around her. "These tourists must spend a fortune to stay here."

"They do—" he started, but his words were abruptly cut off as his entire demeanor shifted.

Peter's gaze locked onto someone across the room. A flicker of recognition passed through his eyes, quickly replaced by something darker. Without a word, he pushed back his chair and strode toward a heavyset man loitering near the dining area.

The second the man spotted Peter, the room seemed to stiffen, tension crackling between them. The man's expression morphed into one of hostility, his finger jabbed pointedly in Peter's direction. Though she couldn't hear the exchange, the man's voice was unmistakable in its intensity, rising in quick, angry bursts, each one more agitated than the last.

Then Peter leaned in, speaking something quietly into the man's ear.

Claire saw it happen—the exact moment the man's bravado crumbled. His face drained of all color, his anger quickly dissolving into something closer to fear.

Then without another word, the man turned and stormed out.

Even as the confrontation ended, a charged silence hung in the air. Peter walked back to her, his movement casual, like nothing had occurred. But Claire couldn't ignore the way his jaw was clenched just a fraction too tightly, a subtle tension betraying his calm exterior.

Claire asked gently, "Everything okay?"

"Just a...former client of mine," he replied, his tone a bit too casual. "Nothing to worry about."

"Client?" she repeated, her curiosity sparking.

"Well, more like a business partner," he clarified with a shrug. "We had a side venture a while back, but...he wasn't the kind of person I wanted to do business with. So I walked away. Clearly, he didn't take it well."

Claire studied him, sensing there was more to the story. But whatever it was, Peter clearly didn't want to discuss it. Despite her lingering curiosity, her excitement to continue their expedition soon pushed the questions away, refocusing her mind on the adventure ahead.

"Where to next?" she asked with a bright smile as they climbed back into the Jeep.

Peter pointed toward a distant herd of zebras. "Let's start there. Afterward, we can head north to a watering hole known for attracting lions. Hopefully, the wildlife will be a bit more cooperative this time."

She grinned. "Perfect."

As the day unfolded, Maasai Mara revealed itself in all its untamed beauty. Every click of Claire's camera captured scenes destined to become lifelong treasures. But it wasn't just the wildlife that captivated her. It was also Peter.

"Did you know giraffes can sleep standing up?" he asked, pointing toward a herd grazing in the distance.

"Seriously?" she asked, lowering her camera for a moment. "That sounds exhausting."

He laughed, the sound warm and unguarded. "I imagine you'd feel the same way if lions were part of your daily worries."

His deep knowledge of the land and its inhabitants, paired with his easy laughter, infused the day with an irresistible energy. The more time she spent with him, the more drawn she felt to his untamed spirit—a spirit as wild and free as the savanna itself.

By late afternoon, Claire stood on the backseat, scanning

the horizon for one last glimpse of wildlife before their departure. Her pulse kicked up when she spotted a dark shape perched high in the branches of a distant acacia tree.

"Peter! Pull over by that tree," she called out, her voice buzzing with the thrill of a potential discovery.

But as they drew closer, her excitement gave way to revulsion.

Draped across a thick limb was the lifeless form of an antelope, its head hanging at an unnatural angle.

"How does that even happen?" she asked, her voice uneasy.

"Leopards," he replied candidly. "They're exceptional climbers. After a kill, they haul their prey into the branches to protect it from scavengers like hyenas. Once it's secured, they can eat in peace or return for it later."

She snapped a few photos of the carcass, her lens lingering on the frenzied swarms of flies that hovered over it. She lowered her camera, sinking back into the passenger seat.

Peter glanced over, noticing her pale expression. "It's not easy to see, is it?"

She shook her head, her voice barely audible. "No, it's not. I mean, I know it's part of the circle of life out here, but…" She trailed off, her gaze drifting back to the carcass. "It's just so raw. So brutal."

He nodded, his tone somber. "It is. But it's also necessary. That carcass is feeding more than just the leopard. It nourishes the soil, the plants, the entire ecosystem. Out here, nothing goes to waste."

She managed a faint nod, though the tightness in her chest remained. "I get it," she murmured. "I just hope I don't have to see it this close again."

The Jeep's engine rumbled to life, and Peter steered toward the reserve's exit. The vast savanna gradually receded behind them, and soon a faint outline of low-lying huts emerged on the horizon. Her pulse quickened, anticipation building as she imagined capturing the charm of this picturesque village through her lens.

Peter parked the Jeep and then glanced at her. "Just remember what I said earlier. Be respectful. Not everyone here will be comfortable with strangers."

"Got it. I'll be careful," she promised, adjusting her camera bag on her shoulder as they stepped out of the Jeep and approached the village.

Almost immediately, an elderly man emerged from one of the huts, his silhouetted figure framed against the glaring sun. His face was a map of deep lines, his flowing white beard swaying with each hurried step. In his hand, he gripped a wooden club.

A rapid stream of unrecognizable words burst from him, each syllable brimming with warning.

Claire flinched, and her eyes darted to Peter, who took a cautious step forward, his hands raised in a gesture of peace.

But the old man's grip on the club only intensified, his knuckles turning white.

No one dared to shift. No one even breathed.

One wrong move…and everything could unravel in an instant.

Chapter 8

The Maasai Village

The old man's scowl deepened as he jabbed a finger toward Claire's bag.

"It's my camera, isn't it?" she whispered to Peter, barely moving her lips.

"Yes, I think so," he murmured, keeping his hands in the air.

Claire's cheeks flushed with embarrassment. She looked at the man, her voice hurried and apologetic. "I'm so sorry. I didn't mean to offend you. I'll put it away." She hoped he understood the sincerity in her tone if not her words.

Moving slowly and cautiously, she backed away, making sure not to startle him. Once at the Jeep, she tucked the camera out of sight.

When she returned, the old man's anger seemed to ease, though a hint of suspicion remained in his eyes. He gave a slow, cautious nod and allowed them to enter the village.

Relieved that the showdown was behind them, they stepped into the bustling community. Claire's senses were instantly overwhelmed by the vibrant tapestry before her: brightly colored garments, wisps of smoke curling into the air, and the shrieks of children darting between the huts.

At first, she was captivated by it all, but as she looked closer, the scene transformed into something else.

Her gaze landed on a young boy, no older than five,

standing apart from the others. An oversized shirt hung limply from his thin, dirt-streaked body. His eyes, red and swollen from infection, glistened with discomfort as he glanced warily at them. A hollow feeling settled deep inside her.

This isn't just poverty, she realized. *It's a desperate fight for survival.*

As they walked up to a round hut, Claire turned to Peter with a hopeful glance. "Do you think they'll let us look inside?"

"You can ask, but I'd rather stay out here," he told her. "I've been inside these native huts plenty of times, and trust me, it's not something I'm eager to experience again."

Although puzzled by his words, her curiosity outweighed her apprehension. Determined to understand more about Maasai culture, she approached an elderly woman standing nearby. "May I go inside?" she asked, motioning toward the hut.

The woman looked at her suspiciously but then shrugged and stepped aside.

Claire ducked through the low doorway, and immediately, a wall of heat slammed into her like an invisible wave, oppressive and stifling. The air seared her throat, and the acrid sting of smoke burned her eyes. Sweat pooled on her forehead and then trickled down her back.

Through the smoky haze, she saw a woman and a teenage girl tending a pot suspended from a rickety rod above a fire. A sheen of perspiration glistened on their faces as they stirred the contents, pausing only to glance up at Claire with quiet curiosity.

Claire offered a small, hesitant smile.

The teenage girl exchanged a quick look with the older woman before giving a shy nod in return. Claire couldn't help but wonder how these women endured such suffocating conditions day after day.

As her eyes finally adjusted to the dim light, the reality of the surroundings became painfully clear. Goats roamed freely inside, their droppings scattered across the floor. Makeshift beds lined the walls, nearly hidden beneath tattered blankets and layers of debris. The mud-coated walls, reinforced with animal dung, trapped the heat and odor, intensifying the claustrophobic atmosphere.

This was nothing like the romanticized vision she had imagined—far from the rustic charm of tribal life shown in documentaries or books. She stood motionless, her illusions crumbling around her.

When she finally stepped outside, the fresh air was a welcome reprieve. She inhaled deeply, letting its crispness fill her lungs.

Before she had time to gather herself, a small girl approached. The child's ribs protruded beneath her threadbare, dirty clothing, and her hollow eyes, dulled by hunger and hardship, were further tormented by the persistent buzz of flies.

Claire crouched slightly, her heart sinking. "Hi there."

The girl didn't reply. She simply held out her hand in a silent plea.

Claire dug into her pockets, searching desperately. Then, her fingers brushed against something small—something insignificant.

A single piece of hard candy.

"Here you go, sweetie," she said, placing the treat gently in the child's hand.

The girl stared at the candy, her expression unreadable. Claire held her breath, suddenly wishing she had more to offer.

Then, the child's face broke into a beaming smile. A delighted squeal escaped her lips as she clutched her tiny treasure and ran off.

As Claire watched her go, the child's joy over something so small rattled her more than anything else she had seen that day.

Once their exploration ended, they made their way back to the Jeep. As the engine hummed to life and the vehicle started moving, Claire cast one last look over her shoulder at the village.

They rode on in silence, but the weight of what she'd seen became too much. "I can't stop thinking about that community," she said, her voice barely above a whisper. "It sits right outside the animal reserve, surrounded by fancy resorts and wealthy tourists. How can everyone just pretend those people aren't suffering?"

"I don't think they're ignoring it," Peter said after a pause, his tone thoughtful. "They see the poverty. But acknowledging it would mean facing their own privilege, and that makes people uncomfortable. It's easier to look away."

She frowned. "But they could spare something for the children in the village. How hard would it be to help?"

"It's not that simple. Tourism brings in jobs and money, sure, but the wealth it generates rarely trickles down to the communities that need it most."

Claire's frustration bubbled over. "That's so unfair! I don't get how people can live with themselves, knowing that kind of suffering is happening right in front of them."

A serious edge crept into Peter's voice. "Claire, think about our own campus. It's a paradise compared to the villages just beyond its gates. How often do you stop and think about the people struggling there?"

His words stung. She thought back to her complaints about the dorms, the classrooms, and even the spotty Wi-Fi. How petty and trivial those grievances felt now, in light of what she had just witnessed.

"You're right," she admitted, her voice softer now. "I've been so caught up in my own inconveniences that I forgot how fortunate I am."

Peter nodded but said nothing more.

As the Jeep bounced along the rugged road, her thoughts drifted back to the little girl. She could still see that bright smile, radiant from something as small as a piece of candy. Such pure joy…despite having so little. The memory tugged at her heart.

Is there more I can do? she wondered. *More ways to show kindness to those who need it most?*

Claire was so lost in her thoughts that she didn't notice the Jeep had stopped. She looked up and saw the familiar surroundings of the campus.

Slowly, she gathered her equipment and turned to Peter. "Thank you. Today meant so much to me. I'll never forget it."

He reached over, his fingers gently brushing against hers as he took her hand. His blue eyes sparkled as he locked onto hers. "It was my pleasure."

A sharp inhale caught in Claire's throat as something unspoken passed between them. The intensity of his gaze, the warmth of his touch—it sent a quiet tremor through her, as if the world had paused for a heartbeat.

Then, slowly, he released her hand, and the moment faded away.

As she walked back to her dorm, the day's events lingered in her mind: the wild, untamed beauty of the savanna, the vibrant Maasai village, and the little girl's hollow eyes. Each experience intertwined, forming something deeper she had yet to fully grasp.

But one thing was certain—the day had changed her. She would never see the world, or her place in it, the same way again.

As she neared her dorm, a sudden cold gust of wind swept across the campus, cutting through her thoughts. She hesitated at the door, glancing over her shoulder. An involuntary shiver shot through her, although she couldn't understand why.

She shook off the unease and stepped inside, unaware that the wind carried more than a chill—it carried a warning. A storm was brewing on the horizon, one that would test her strength and resilience in ways she could never have imagined.

And it was already closing in.

Chapter 9

Mystery Behind the Shed

In the days that followed her excursion, Claire began to see the world through a different lens. Gratitude gently replaced her former grumblings, and even the simplest moments felt richer.

She found herself appreciating the vibrant flowers that lined the pathways, the camaraderie of the women she worked with in the kitchen, and the refreshing breeze that swept through the classrooms on hot afternoons. Even Peter's glances seemed to carry more weight now. Each time his blue eyes met hers during class, her heart skipped a beat.

One afternoon after her last class, Claire wandered to the far edge of the campus—a quiet spot she had never explored before. Beneath the sprawling branches of a tree, she found a simple wooden bench. With the sun warming her face, she settled down, savoring the moment.

Then, a movement in the distance caught her eye.

Near a maintenance shed, Daniel stood rigid, his eyes darting around as if searching for something…or someone. His usual easygoing energy seemed to be missing, replaced by an edge of restlessness.

"Daniel!" she called out instinctively.

He didn't seem to hear her.

Before she could try again, a campus security guard appeared, striding toward him with purpose. The guard's severe demeanor was anything but friendly, and she worried that Daniel might be in trouble.

But to her surprise, the two men exchanged a brief nod and then disappeared behind the shed. Claire waited. She expected Daniel to emerge quickly, but the seconds stretched into minutes, and still nothing.

Finally, she couldn't take it any longer. She had to find out what was happening.

She rose from the bench and headed toward the shed. As she approached, low voices carried through the air.

She crept forward and peeked around the corner. Daniel and the security guard stood twenty feet away, their stiff postures and hushed tones betraying the tension between them.

She swung back around, pressing her back against the cold metal wall of the shed, hoping they hadn't seen her.

"I can't believe you're raising the price on me!" she heard Daniel exclaim, his voice cracking with desperation. "That's a ridiculous amount of money. You know I don't have that!"

The guard's reply was cool, almost mocking. "These things don't come cheap, kid. You Americans always want the goods but cry about the price. If you couldn't afford it, you wouldn't be in Kenya."

"But I'm not some rich tourist," Daniel protested. "I'm a student!"

The guard let out a low, derisive chuckle. "A poor student? Sure you are. And yet here you are, sniffing around for something as valuable as a tusk. There's a reason they're contraband, you know. Only the wealthy or the stupid try to buy them on the black market. You want it? You'll pay the new price. No exceptions."

Claire clamped a hand over her mouth, suppressing a gasp. *A tusk? Contraband? Black market?* The words rang in her ears, almost too surreal to process. *Daniel couldn't be involved in something like that. Right?*

"It's none of your business why I want it!" Daniel snapped, his voice sharp, unrecognizably angry. "We had a deal. I'll pay what we agreed on. No more."

This wasn't the Daniel she knew. His voice held a jagged edge—something almost dangerous. Her mind raced, trying to piece together what had pushed him to this point, desperate to find a way to stop him before it was too late.

Then, an idea struck her. *I need proof of this meeting.*

If she could gather evidence, she'd have something concrete to confront him with—something to expose whatever dark path he was on.

Fumbling inside her bag, she pulled out her phone and pressed record. Her fingers quivered as she angled it around the corner, hoping the microphone would pick up their voices.

"The price has gone up," the guard countered. "If you can't pay, you're wasting my time. But if you want it badly enough, you'll figure it out." He paused, then he added coldly, "Or else."

Daniel's next words sliced through the air, cold and sharp as a knife.

"Are you threatening me?" His voice was low, each word edged with steel. "Because if I were you…I'd think twice."

"I'm just telling you how it is," the guard shot back.

A strained silence stretched between them. Then she heard a long exhale.

"Fine," Daniel said, his voice clipped. "I'll get the extra money. When and where?"

The guard's voice dropped to a growl. "I'll set up a meeting with my boss. He'll bring the item, and you'll bring the *full* payment. But let me warn you," he added, his tone turning icy. "My boss is not someone you want to cross. He's a dangerous man, so bring every last penny, or you'll regret it."

Claire stopped the recording and backed away from the shed, moving with careful, silent steps. Then, once she was a safe distance away, she broke into a sprint, her lungs burning as she ran toward her dorm. The magnitude of what she had just heard bore down on her, a relentless pressure squeezing her lungs like a vice.

By the time she slipped inside her empty dorm, she was

gulping for air. She forced deep breaths, but it did little to calm the storm raging in her mind.

Everything she heard pointed toward one chilling conclusion: Daniel was trying to buy an elephant tusk on the black market. Not only was it illegal in Kenya, but it was a death sentence for the majestic creature. But why?

She sank onto her bed, her thoughts spinning. Daniel had confided in her recently about his financial struggles. Was he planning to sell it? Could he really be that desperate?

The consequences for Daniel terrified her. Expulsion, arrest, a ruined future—it could all come crashing down on him.

And if that wasn't bad enough, an image flashed in her mind of an elephant, its massive body lifeless, its tusks hacked away in the brutal reality of the ivory trade.

She buried her head in her hands, trapped between two impossible choices: expose what she'd heard and risk destroying Daniel's life—and their friendship—or stay silent and allow an innocent animal to suffer.

No matter what she chose, someone would pay the price.

Think, she urged herself. *What should I do?*

Her fingers hovered over her phone, the recording waiting—a secret ready to reveal everything. Should she confront Daniel with it? Or share it with someone else—someone who could help her make sense of it?

"Claire?"

The sound of her name made her jump so violently that her phone nearly slipped from her grasp. Her breath caught as she whipped around to face him.

Daniel stood at the doorway, his relaxed smile masking the secrets she knew he was hiding.

"You busy?"

She cleared her throat, hoping it disguised the uneasiness in her voice. "Oh, hey, Daniel. I...I was just about to lie down for a bit."

If he noticed the tremor in her voice, he didn't react. Instead, he leaned nonchalantly against the doorframe, his usual easygoing energy on full display, like this was just another ordinary evening.

"Well, if you're not too tired, want to grab dinner? Rachel's already at the dining hall."

Dinner. With him. After what I just heard?

Every muscle in her body stiffened. He looked the same and sounded the same, but she couldn't forget what she had just overheard. The cold exchange. The veiled threats. The deal he was making.

She shook her head quickly, willing her voice to stay even. "No, thanks. I'm not hungry."

Daniel narrowed his eyes playfully. "Not hungry?" He gasped dramatically. "Who are you, and what have you done with Claire?" A grin spread across his face as he let out a chuckle.

She forced a smile. "No, really. I'll just grab a snack later."

With a casual shrug, he said, "Alright." He turned toward the door, tossing a final, carefree farewell over his shoulder. "See you later."

The second he stepped away, she shot to her feet. She couldn't sit on this information any longer. She needed someone who knew the guards, understood the inner workings of the college, and could help her sort out this mess.

She needed Peter.

She took a step toward the door, then froze as she remembered that students weren't allowed in staff quarters. But even as the rule surfaced in her mind, she felt a surge of defiance.

Forget the rules! This is too important.

Before doubt could take hold, she burst through the door and into the night, sprinting across campus.

She didn't care about the consequences.

Not anymore.

Chapter 10

The Professor's Advice

Claire's fist slammed against the wooden door of Peter's cottage, each pound echoing her beating heart.

The door swung open, and Peter appeared. "Claire?" His gaze swept over her flushed face, taking in her wild eyes and shaky hands. "What's wrong?"

"It's Daniel," she gasped, trying to control her breathing. "I think he's in serious trouble! I overheard him talking to a security guard about...about buying an elephant tusk."

Peter's expression shifted instantly, darkening like a gathering storm. Without hesitation, he stepped aside. "Come in. Sit down," he said, his voice urgent. "Tell me everything."

She took a seat and recounted the conversation she'd overheard, her words tumbling out in a rush. When she finally finished, Peter leaned back, his face grim.

"That could indeed be serious. The illegal ivory trade is a major problem in Kenya, and those involved in it can be... dangerous. If Daniel's caught up in something like that, well, the consequences could be disastrous."

"What should I do?" she asked.

He hesitated for a moment, his expression thoughtful. "Daniel seems like a good person, and the guard you described sounds like Samuel, someone I know personally. Are you absolutely certain about what you heard?"

"I...I heard the guard say something about an elephant

tusk," she replied, though uncertainty crept into her mind as she replayed the conversation in her mind. Had she heard that, or was she just piecing things together out of suspicion?

Peter tilted his head slightly, his gaze penetrating. "Are you certain? Conversations can sound different when you're only hearing part of them."

"I'm not sure about the elephant part," she admitted, her voice weaker now. "But I swear I heard *tusk*."

"It's easy to mishear things, especially if you are nervous or distracted. Could it have been about something else?"

She opened her mouth to argue, but then it hit her. "Wait!" she blurted out. "I recorded part of it!" Her fingers trembled as she scrolled through her files, finally pressing play.

The audio crackled to life, but the voices were faint, muffled under layers of static. They strained to make out a few words—"price," "meeting," "boss," and "dangerous."

Peter let out a slow exhale. "That's not much to go on, is it?"

This was supposed to be her smoking gun. But now, it felt frustratingly inadequate. Worse, there was no mention of a tusk, the very word that had fueled her suspicions in the first place.

"But doesn't it still seem shady to you?" she pressed him, unwilling to let go just yet. "I heard the guard talk about raising the price, there were threats, and you heard him say *dangerous*!"

He shook his head. "It sounds like some sort of deal, sure. But that doesn't necessarily make it illegal. It could just as easily be about a wood carving or an African drum."

She scoffed. "I don't think people dealing in wood carvings are usually dangerous."

He let out a measured breath. "Probably not, but without real evidence, jumping to conclusions could have serious consequences. Think about it. Do you honestly believe Daniel is capable of doing something like this?"

The question landed harder than she expected. "No," she admitted. "He's always been honest. Maybe a little reckless, but not…this."

He nodded. "Exactly. So unless you have real proof, it's best to let this go. Otherwise, you might end up hurting an innocent friend."

Every instinct in her told her that something about the incident wasn't right. But Peter's calm logic was hard to argue with.

"Alright," she finally relented. "If you think it's best, I'll drop it."

Peter flashed her a warm, reassuring smile. "Good. You're making the right decision. Rumors, even unintentional ones, can ruin someone's life. So let's keep this between us for now, okay?"

Then, with a chuckle, he leaned back and flashed her a sly grin. "Next time I see Samuel, I'll ask how his side gig selling overpriced wood carvings is going."

She attempted to mirror his humor with a smile of her own, but it fell flat. As she stood to leave, he reached out and clasped her hand, stopping her progress.

"Wait, Claire," he said, his voice soft yet insistent. "I know this hasn't been easy for you. Why don't you stay a while? You look upset, and we could talk more, just to put your mind at ease."

His fingers tightened slightly, not enough to be forceful, but enough to hold her attention. Though his touch remained gentle, there was an undercurrent to it—something that left her feeling slightly uneasy.

"Thank you, but students aren't allowed in staff housing," she reminded him as she gently pulled her hand free. "Besides, it's late, and I should really get back."

"I'm sure no one would object," he responded, his tone persistent. "Are you sure you don't want to stay? Just for a little while longer?"

His piercing blue eyes held hers, their intensity almost hypnotic. The pull was subtle but unmistakable. For a brief moment, her resolve wavered. *What harm could it do if I stayed?* The thought slipped into her mind like a whisper.

But just as quickly, it was gone.

"No, I need to go," she replied, firmer now, stepping back.

Something in his expression shifted—the faintest hint of irritation, masked so quickly that she questioned whether it had been there at all.

"If you must," he mumbled, following her to the door.

When Claire stepped outside, she filled her lungs with the crisp air. It grounded her, clearing the strange fog that had crept in while she was inside. With that breath came certainty—leaving had been the right choice. Peter's sudden invitation had felt like venturing too close to a boundary she wasn't ready to cross.

She started toward her dorm, but doubt wrapped around her thoughts like choking weeds. Peter had given her a rational explanation, but reason alone couldn't erase the sharp tension in the voices she had overheard. Daniel's desperation had been real, and the guard's voice had an unmistakable edge of menace. That confrontation wasn't just puzzling; it carried an implication of something far darker.

Her steps slowed. She replayed her conversation with Daniel before coming to see Peter—the effortless way he joked, the warmth of his smile, oblivious to her suspicions. If she stayed silent, if she pretended she hadn't heard anything, she was sure it would create a rift between them.

From now on, every interaction would feel strained, and every shared moment would be overshadowed by unspoken doubt. Their friendship would fracture, piece by piece, until nothing was left.

No. I refuse to let that happen.

She stopped and turned, casting one last glance at Peter's cottage, its silhouette lost to the encroaching night. He had wanted her to let it go—to walk away. But she knew she couldn't.

She squared her shoulders, shaking off any hesitation as determination took hold.

"If real proof is what he wants, then that's what I'll get," she declared.

This had moved beyond mere curiosity. Now, it was about Daniel. About truth. About doing what was right.

One thing was certain—there was *no* walking away now.

Chapter 11

The Trip to Narok

As Claire woke the next morning, fragments of Daniel's hushed meeting with the guard replayed in her mind like a broken record.

If it had been just an innocent conversation, why all the secrecy? But if it wasn't…the alternative was far worse. Daniel could be in way over his head, tangled in something dangerous.

Either way, she knew she couldn't ignore it. She had to get to the bottom of it.

By the time she made it to the dining hall, however, her resolve had already begun to crack. *How do I uncover the truth when I don't know where to start?*

At the breakfast table, Rachel chatted away, her voice light and animated, but Claire barely registered the conversation. She sat staring at her plate, idly pushing her eggs around.

She wasn't sure she was ready to confront Daniel or admit she'd been eavesdropping. And what if she'd misinterpreted the conversation? She couldn't risk accusing him unfairly.

With a quiet sigh, she set her fork down, her appetite smothered by uncertainty.

She looked up to find Daniel acting like his usual self —engaged, cracking jokes. But as the minutes passed, a subtle change took place. His fingers drummed against his coffee cup, and his eyes kept darting toward the entrance, like he was expecting someone.

Claire studied him closely, trying to understand why he seemed so on edge.

When Rachel noticed she was the only one talking, she glanced between them. "Okay, what's up with you two? You're both acting...weird."

"What makes you say that?" Daniel asked, his voice calm, but Claire noticed a faint twitch in his jaw.

Rachel leaned forward. "Well, for starters, you keep checking the door like you have somewhere better to be. And you've been absently stirring that coffee for, what—ten minutes now?" She gestured toward his cup just as he took a sip. "Cold, right?"

Daniel blinked, then forced a chuckle, setting his mug down. "Guess I got lost in thought." He stretched his arms overhead with a lazy grin. "Relax, Rach. I'm...just tired."

Rachel's gaze then switched to Claire. "And you? You've hardly said a word, and you haven't eaten a single bite. Plus, you skipped dinner last night."

Claire shifted in her seat, suddenly aware of how still she had been. "I'm fine. Just not a fan of the eggs this morning," she replied, but the words felt brittle, as if they might snap beneath the burden of the truth.

Rachel didn't look convinced. "Yeah, that totally explains the weird vibes."

Daniel let out an exaggerated sigh. "Geez. Can't a guy drink his coffee in peace?"

Rachel shook her head, muttering, "You two are impossible." With a sigh, she grabbed her coffee. "Fine, keep your little secrets. But just so you know, I'm onto you."

Claire opened her mouth to say something to her, but the words refused to come. The situation was a chaotic mess, her mind reeling with doubt and confusion.

She clenched her fists under the table. *Uncover the truth? Who am I kidding? I'm no closer now than I was last night!*

A sudden tap on her shoulder made Claire jump. She spun around to find two women from the kitchen standing behind her.

"Hi, Claire," one of them spoke brightly. "We're heading to Narok this morning for a supply run. Would you like to join us? We could use your help."

The invitation caught her off guard, but the idea of a trip to Narok immediately sparked her interest. Maybe stepping away for a while would help her see things more clearly—and decide what to do about Daniel.

"I'd love to," she declared, her voice lighter than she'd felt all morning. Then, noticing a hint of longing in Rachel's expression, she turned back to the women. "Would it be alright if my friend joined us?"

The women exchanged a glance before nodding. "Of course. We can always use an extra pair of hands."

Rachel's face lit up instantly as she grabbed her things and followed Claire and the women through the kitchen toward the waiting truck.

"I've heard so much about Narok!" Rachel gushed. "The markets, the shops, the restaurants—everything sounds amazing! And did you know it has the most churches in the entire region? I don't even mind skipping class for this!"

An hour later, the truck rolled into Narok, and Claire felt like she had stepped into another world.

The city pulsed with vibrant energy where sleek malls and high-rise apartments stood side by side with tribesmen herding their cattle through the streets. Cars honked incessantly, and motorcycles rumbled as they zigzagged through traffic.

The truck finally stopped in front of a sprawling open-air market. Rows of makeshift stalls stretched in every direction, their colorful displays glinting under the bright sun. Vendors called out their wares in a flurry of overlapping voices, bargaining with customers.

One of the women outlined the plan. "Claire, you'll come with us as we barter at different shops. They only speak Maa or Swahili, so your job will be to help carry the supplies back to the truck."

"Sounds good!" she responded, her anticipation building.

The woman then addressed Rachel. "Can you stay here and watch the supplies? Leaving them unattended wouldn't be a good idea."

A big grin spread across Rachel's face. "You got it. I'll guard them with my life!"

Claire followed the women into the fray, weaving through the throngs of people, the pungent scent of cooked meat and spices filling the air.

She lugged heavy loads of rice, vegetables, and meat back and forth between the vendors and the truck. The exertion was exhausting, but it gave her the distraction she needed. For the first time in days, the weight of her worries grew lighter, if only for a little while.

By the time the shopping was complete, Claire and the women returned to Rachel, who had patiently stood watch over the growing pile of goods. Grateful for their efforts, the women offered to buy them lunch, a gesture the girls eagerly accepted.

They drove to a gleaming, gated mall complex and chose a restaurant with inviting outdoor seating. As they waited for their food, Rachel, still buzzing from the market experience, pulled a beaded bracelet from her bag.

"I bought this from a guy who came up to me while I was guarding the truck," she announced proudly. "Isn't it gorgeous?"

Claire's eyes lit up as she leaned closer to admire the intricate beadwork. "It's beautiful! Do you think I could find something like it?"

"Maybe. Why don't you ask the ladies?"

Claire approached one of their companions. "Would it be alright if we went to a jewelry shop after lunch?"

The woman shook her head apologetically. "I'm sorry, but we need to head straight back to campus to store the supplies. But there's a shop just down the road that sells local jewelry and crafts. Why don't you girls check it out while we wait for our food?"

Eager to find a keepsake, Claire and Rachel hurried to

the store. True to the woman's description, it was filled with a stunning array of Maasai creations: beaded jewelry, vibrant fabrics, and intricate crafts. Claire checked out the bold patterns, excitement building as she searched for the perfect piece.

She finally settled on a bracelet in the colors of the Kenyan flag and moved toward the counter to pay. As she approached, the door creaked open.

A scruffy redheaded man stepped inside. He seemed out of place with his rumpled clothes and tense posture. He moved among the shelves, but there was a restless energy to his browsing, an agitated edge that made Claire uneasy.

She told herself she was imagining things—until she glimpsed his reflection in a display case.

His eyes weren't scanning the merchandise.

They were focused on *them*.

Chapter 12

The Redheaded Man

Claire's fingers grasped the bracelet a little tighter.

She turned, casting another glance at the man. He quickly averted his gaze—but not fast enough.

She swallowed against the rising panic. *How long has he been watching us?*

Her hands shook as she fumbled for the money. She shoved the payment across the counter, barely registering the transaction, and then turned quickly to Rachel.

"Let's go," she whispered.

They rushed back to the restaurant. When lunch arrived, the rich aroma of beef stew and freshly made chapati eased her nerves. For the first time, she felt herself relax...until a sudden chill pricked the back of her neck.

Intuition urged her to look around.

Across the restaurant, in the dim corner, sat the redheaded man. A steaming cup of tea rested in his hands, his posture deceptively relaxed. But his eyes told a different story—piercing, unsettling, and locked onto her with an almost savage intensity.

She fought to steady herself. *He's followed us here!*

She leaned in closer to Rachel, lowering her voice. "Rachel. See that man with the red hair?"

Rachel followed her friend's subtle nod. "Yeah, I see him. What about him?"

"Don't stare!" Claire hissed. "He was in the store with us earlier."

Rachel raised an eyebrow, glancing at the man again. "Okay… and?"

"I think he followed us here," she mumbled, her voice barely audible.

Rachel snorted softly, trying to stifle a laugh. "Or maybe he just really likes tea. I mean, this *is* a restaurant."

She scowled. "I'm serious. He's *watching* us!"

Rachel sighed and leaned back, giving the man a more deliberate once-over. "Okay, but don't you think you're overreacting? Why would some random guy follow us around Narok? That's kind of a leap."

Claire hesitated, reluctant to admit it, but Rachel had a point. Was she just being paranoid?

"Maybe you're right," she said slowly. "It's just…lately, it seems like things aren't as they appear."

Rachel's playful grin faded slightly. "That sounds ominous. Want to talk about it? Because since yesterday, you've been acting like the weight of the world is on your shoulders. Seriously, what's going on?"

Claire considered telling her everything. But what if she was wrong? If she shared her suspicions now, she'd only stir up doubt in Rachel's mind about Daniel—without any proof to back it up."

"It's nothing, really," she said, forcing a smile. "I know I've been stressed, but I promise, I'll figure it out."

Hoping to shift the conversation, Claire gestured toward the bustling street outside the restaurant. "Isn't this city amazing? I mean, look at all this energy. It's nothing like back home."

Skepticism clouded Rachel's expression. For a moment, it looked like she might press further, but then she sighed, as if deciding it wasn't worth the fight. "Yeah, it's amazing."

After a brief pause, Rachel's mood shifted, and she brightened. "Hey, did you see that church on the corner before we got here? Do you think the ladies would mind if we stopped by for a quick look before heading back?"

Claire shook her head. "They said we had to head straight back after lunch, remember?" Then, noticing Rachel's expression, she asked, "What's so special about visiting a church, anyway?"

Rachel's face softened, her voice dropping to a more thoughtful tone. "It's not just a building to me. Being in the house of God...well, it just feels different. Peaceful, you know?"

Claire felt the sincerity in her friend's words. It was more than a casual remark; there was a deep, heartfelt devotion behind it.

"Do you really think a loving God cares about us?" she asked her friend. "It's hard for me to believe that when there's so much suffering in the world."

Rachel reached across the table and placed a soothing hand on Claire's. "I get that; that's a feeling many share. I know you have been struggling since your brother's death, but just because he died doesn't mean that God didn't care about him. We can't always see the bigger picture, so sometimes we just have to trust Him."

"I miss my brother so much, Rachel," she murmured. "So believing that God loves me after that...it just feels... impossible."

Rachel gave her hand a comforting squeeze. "I can't even imagine your pain, but I truly believe that God's love is greater than what we can understand. Even in our darkest times, He's there, offering comfort and guidance."

"How do you trust in something you don't understand?" Claire asked.

"That's what faith is. It's trusting God even when we don't have all the answers. It's a journey, and God understands our doubts and struggles. He'll be waiting for you, Claire...once you realize He never left."

The warmth of Rachel's words lingered as they finished their meal, creating a comforting backdrop to their time together.

As they prepared to leave, Claire's gaze drifted back to the mysterious man's table. It was conspicuously empty now, but his absence did little to ease her nerves.

The unsettling feeling that he had followed them refused to let go. She tried to brush it off, telling herself it was all in her head. But no matter how much she replayed it, she felt sure that he wasn't just a random passerby in Narok. He had followed them intentionally.

His face flashed before her again—his sharp, calculating gaze, dissecting her every move.

Then the realization hit her like a gut punch, and a sudden chill rippled through her body.

He hadn't been following *them*.

He'd only been watching *her*.

Chapter 13

Undeniable Proof

Sleep didn't come easily that night. Every time Claire closed her eyes, the redheaded man's piercing gaze surfaced—cold and calculating.

She felt utterly powerless under his scrutiny, as if she were prey caught in a predator's sights. Each time she tried to push him from her mind, his stare would resurface, sharper and more menacing.

Then her thoughts would spiral back to Daniel's secretive meeting with the guard. The two events twisted together in a restless loop, like two threads slowly suffocating her thoughts, each feeding the other, amplifying her anxiety.

Two mysteries in two days—was it coincidence, or something more?

Lying awake, an idea began to take shape. Oddly enough, it was the man's actions that sparked it. If Daniel was hiding something, the only way to uncover the truth was to shadow him—observe, listen, and stay close.

By morning, she was ready. Drawing inspiration from her favorite detective novels, she slipped into the role of an amateur sleuth. Every shared meal, joint morning run, walk to class, and late-night study session became an opportunity for silent observation. She scrutinized Daniel's every word and gesture, searching for anything that might explain his clandestine meeting, or expose a darker truth hidden beneath his easy going façade.

But Daniel remained the same warm, considerate, and charming friend he had always been. His kindness felt genuine, not an act. Eventually, she began to doubt herself, wondering if she had misjudged him entirely.

One afternoon at lunch, with only Daniel seated across from her, Claire decided it was time to be more direct.

"Hey, Daniel," she said, trying to keep her tone light.

"Hmm," he mumbled, mid-bite.

She leaned in, watching his face closely. "I thought I saw you last week, near the far end of campus while I was taking a walk. What were you doing way over there?"

Daniel swallowed, then glanced up, considering. "Last Tuesday?" He nodded like he was piecing it together. "Oh yeah. I was meeting with Samuel, one of the guards. I needed his help finding something."

Her pulse quickened. "Finding what?"

"Just a keepsake. Samuel's sister makes Maasai jewelry, and I thought a wedding necklace would be a nice gift for my mom."

She blinked. "A *wedding* necklace?"

"They're hard to find," he explained. "I figured Samuel might know if his sister had one for sale."

Something about his answer didn't feel right. The ease of it. The way it fit too neatly into place. Still, she forced a polite smile. "Did you manage to get one?"

"Nope, all out. Back to the drawing board, I guess. Unless…" He gave her a playful look. "You wouldn't happen to know a secret jewelry source, would you?"

Claire tried to smile. "No, sorry."

She wanted to believe him. She *needed* to believe him. But the tense conversation behind the shed didn't line up with his casual, offhand explanation.

As she walked out of the cafeteria, frustration simmered. She was no closer to the truth than when she'd started.

By the end of the week, she knew she couldn't put off

confronting Daniel any longer. Her attempts at sleuthing had gotten her nowhere, and a possibility she had been avoiding resurfaced—Peter might have been right all along.

When she and Rachel stepped into the dining hall for dinner, Daniel wasn't there. Claire instinctively scanned the room, a wave of unexpected worry settling in. Could he be meeting with Samuel again?

"You okay?" Rachel's voice cut through her thoughts.

Claire barely heard her. She mumbled an excuse and hurried out, racing back to the maintenance shed.

Don't let him be there. Don't let him be there! The silent plea repeated in her mind, even as a deep part of her already knew the truth.

She slowed her steps as she neared the building, pressing herself against the cold, metal wall. Her heart pounded so violently she feared someone might hear it.

She stole a glance around the corner—

And her stomach dropped like a stone.

There stood Daniel, tense and rigid, his hands fidgeting at his sides. Beside him, Samuel's intense gaze swept the area like a hawk, constantly alert. But it was the third man who unsettled her the most. Unfamiliar. Imposing. His very presence radiated authority.

The boss.

She strained to hear them, but their words were lost in the distance.

All she could think about was getting real proof—something irrefutable, something no one could deny.

Just one clear photo, she told herself, her fingers closing in around her phone. *That's all I need.*

Carefully, she angled her phone around the corner for a blind shot and pressed the white button. She checked the screen. Blurry. Distant. Useless.

She had to get closer.

Summoning every ounce of courage, she edged around the corner, exposing her presence. She pressed her back against the wall of the shed as she moved with agonizing slowness. The air felt charged, the danger lurking just feet away.

What am I doing? The thought tore through her mind like a scream. *This is insane!*

Then she saw it.

The third man lifted something from the shadows. The gleaming smooth curve of ivory caught the dim light like a sinister trophy.

A surge of vindication flooded her, but it quickly gave way to horror as she watched Daniel lean in, his fingers brushing the tusk's curve with an almost clinical detachment. But it was his eyes that chilled her to the bone—a dark hunger smoldered there, a side of him she'd never seen before.

But there was no time to process; no time to think. Her world narrowed to a single, desperate task: capture the proof.

She raised her phone, zoomed in, and pressed the button.

Click.

The shutter sound was barely a whisper, but Samuel's head snapped toward her hiding spot.

"Someone's here," he hissed.

Claire pressed herself deeper into the shadows, willing herself to vanish.

But then Samuel's gaze locked onto hers. For a split second, they stared at each other—

The hunter and the hunted.

Chapter 14

Caught in the Crosshairs

Claire bolted into a desperate sprint, but she didn't dare look back. Nothing mattered except escape.

Then came the sound she feared most.

Thud. Thud. Thud.

Footsteps. Gaining on her.

Horrified, she pushed herself faster, frantically searching for a place to hide.

Then—disaster.

Her foot caught on a patch of uneven ground, and she crashed down hard. A stinging stab shot through her palms and knees. She tried to stand up, but a rough hand clamped around her wrist like a steel trap.

A figure crouched down, and a low, menacing growl vibrated near her ear. "And just where do you think you're going?"

She looked up and saw Samuel's scowling face. The fury in his eyes sent a bolt of terror through her.

"No answer?" he snarled. "I saw you back at the shed. You were spying on us." His grip intensified, sending a shooting pain up her arm.

"N-no! I wasn't!" she gasped, her voice breaking.

Samuel's contempt deepened. "Liar. What do you know? What did you see?"

Before she could stutter out another feeble denial, a sharp

voice sliced through the tension.

"What's going on here?"

Daniel emerged from the shadows, his chest rising and falling as though he'd been running. His eyes, blazing with intensity, locked onto Samuel.

But Samuel didn't flinch. "I heard a camera click," he growled. "She took a picture of us."

Thinking fast, Claire blurted out, "No! I...I was just taking a walk! I tripped, that's all."

Daniel's expression darkened as he looked at Samuel. He stepped forward, his voice low and lethal.

"Let. Her. Go."

Samuel's fingers tightened instead, as if testing his limits. But when Daniel closed the distance between them, his posture rigid with a silent warning, Samuel finally released her with a sharp huff.

"Fine," Samuel muttered. "Let's see what *you* can get out of her."

Daniel immediately turned to Claire, his voice softer. "Are you okay?"

She clung to his arm for balance. "No. I, um, think I hurt my knee," she replied, wincing for effect as she clutched at her kneecap.

Daniel knelt before her, his hands gentle as he brushed a pebble from her scraped knee. His voice was quieter now, almost gentle. "It looks bad. Come on, I'll take you to the infirmary."

"Yes," she countered. "The infirmary." *Anywhere but here.*

Daniel offered his arm for support, and Claire leaned into him, exaggerating a limp as they walked away. She could feel Samuel's eyes burning into her back, her skin crawling under their weight. But she didn't look back, willing herself not to react.

Only when they made it to a quiet, deserted stretch of the path did Daniel pull his arm free. For a moment, neither of them spoke. The silence between them was thick and charged.

Finally, Claire couldn't hold back. "I know what you're

doing," she exclaimed, her voice shaking with anger and frustration. "You should not be dealing with those men!"

"How could you possibly know what I'm doing?" he asked, almost dismissively.

"Because I overheard you." The accusation burned in her throat. "Last week, when you met with Samuel, I heard everything. You weren't buying a necklace, were you? You were after a tusk."

Daniel let out a slow, heavy sigh, dragging a hand through his hair. "Claire, I wish you hadn't heard that," he muttered, glancing away. "You don't understand. You could ruin everything."

"Ruin everything?" she shot back, her voice rising. "Do you even realize how reckless this is? Or how dangerous these people are?"

A muscle tensed in Daniel's jaw. "I don't need a lecture from you, Claire. I know exactly what I'm doing." His voice carried an edge that made her flinch.

"Do you?" she demanded, tears stinging her eyes. "Because all I see is you working with criminals who slaughter innocent animals!"

For the first time, Daniel faltered. A shadow passed across his face—not anger, but something deeper, something broken. But just as quickly, it was gone—replaced by a cool, unreadable expression.

"Claire, you need to walk away from this," he replied sharply. "Because if you don't, I can't promise you'll be safe."

Her stomach twisted at the warning in his tone. "Is that a threat?"

"No." His voice softened, but just barely. "It's the truth. Please, just trust me on this."

"Trust you?" she choked out, her voice cracking. "How can I trust you when you've lied to me?"

"Listen to me, Claire." His voice was quieter now. "If you care about me, about our friendship, you'll let this go. If you don't, you *will* be in danger."

His gaze lingered on hers for a fraction of a second, clouded with something she couldn't decipher. "One day," he finally mumbled, "you'll understand."

Without another word, he walked away, his silhouette disappearing into the night, leaving Claire standing there—stunned, hurt, and more confused than ever.

Daniel's betrayal cut deep, carving a hollow ache in her chest. And yet, he had stepped in, shielding her from Samuel's wrath—and possibly something far worse.

The paradox of him, both the one who wounded her and the one who protected her, was a riddle that defied logic. Her legs buckled from the weight of it all, and she collapsed onto a nearby bench.

She had gambled everything to get that photo. And lost.

She hadn't just witnessed an illegal deal—she was in the crosshairs now. And the people she'd crossed weren't the forgiving type.

Something was coming for her, closing in fast. She just didn't know if she could outrun it.

Chapter 15

Exposed

Claire peered toward the empty, unlit path where Daniel had vanished, the darkness swallowing every trace of him, leaving nothing but the echo of his betrayal.

She had uncovered the truth—seen the tusk, witnessed the poachers' secretive exchange—but at what cost? She had become tangled in something far bigger than she'd ever imagined.

But she still had the evidence, proof of what she had seen, captured in a single frame.

Her fingers trembled as she pulled out her phone, the screen's pale glow casting sharp shadows across her face. The photo filled the display: Daniel, Samuel, and a wiry man with a bushy gray beard, his features carved from stone. In his hand—the damning evidence. A gleaming ivory tusk.

The image was undeniable. Irrefutable. And if they knew she had it, she wouldn't just be in their sights—she'd be the target.

A sharp breath hitched in her throat as the realization struck. The photo wasn't just evidence—it was a death sentence. The poachers wouldn't stop until it was in their hands.

But what if I expose them first?

She couldn't waste another second. Claire sprang to her feet and rushed back to her dorm.

Once inside, she moved quickly, transferring the photo

to her laptop. Each keystroke echoed like a drumbeat in the stillness. Just to be safe, she copied it onto a flash drive, her fingers trembling as she completed the task.

Two copies. *But is that enough?*

Her gaze darted around the room, searching for a hiding place. She found a crack in the far wall. Perfect. Snatching her tweezers, she slid the flash drive deep into the crevice, shoving it in until it disappeared.

With the evidence safely secure, her next move was clear. She had to go back to Peter.

The incriminating evidence was too compelling for him to ignore this time. And, with any luck, he could help her expose the poaching ring before it was too late.

She grabbed her phone and flew out the door.

A sense of déjà vu crept over her as she ran across the campus, her mind flashing back to that night a week ago when she had gone to his cottage for help.

But this time, the fear was different. Darker. Heavier. Every rustle of leaves revved up her pulse, every distant footstep made her glance over her shoulder, searching for unseen threats.

Someone could be watching her.

Someone could be following her.

By the time she reached Peter's door, her whole body was trembling. Her knuckles hammered against the wood, the sound ricocheting through the stillness. She kept pounding. Harder. Faster.

Finally, the door cracked open, revealing Peter's startled face. "Claire?" His voice was stern at first, but as his eyes met hers, the irritation softened into something gentler. "What's going on?"

She held up her phone. "Peter, I have real proof! About the black market on campus!"

His brows shot up, his expression shifting to surprise. He stepped aside quickly, his voice measured but urgent. "Black market? Are you serious?" He shut the door firmly behind her.

Claire launched into her story. She described the second

secret meeting, the imposing third man, and the incriminating photo. She pulled up the image and handed him the phone.

He took it, his face tensed as he examined it. He was quiet for a long time, as if weighing the gravity of the situation.

"This is…" He exhaled, his fingers zooming in on the tusk. "…serious. There's something much bigger happening here than I thought."

"And now Samuel knows I took a picture of them." The words caught in her throat. "I…I think I've put myself in danger!"

He leaned in slightly, his voice dropping into something low and reassuring. "Claire, I understand you're scared, and you have every right to be. I'm sorry I didn't believe you the first time. But I don't really think they'd target a student. Not here on campus. You'll be safe, I promise."

Her voice barely rose above a whisper. "But Daniel…what if they go after him?"

Peter sighed heavily, like the burden of responsibility had settled onto his shoulders. "You're right. If Daniel's involved, he's in way over his head. But don't worry, I'll take this straight to the Dean." He handed Claire her phone. "Can you send me the photo? I'll need it for my report."

Claire nodded and quickly attached the image to an email and sent it.

Peter gave her an encouraging smile, the kind that made her feel like she wasn't alone in this. "The Dean will know how to handle this. And I'll vouch for Daniel, explain how he was likely coerced by these men. He shouldn't face any serious consequences."

She exhaled in relief. "Really? You think he'll be okay?"

"I'm certain," he replied warmly. He reached out, resting a hand gently on hers. "You did the right thing by coming to me, Claire. Most people wouldn't have been brave enough."

The praise brought a faint flush to her cheeks, and she nodded.

Then his expression shifted, ever so slightly. "Claire, listen carefully. Don't share this with anyone, not until we hear back from the Dean. The last thing we need is for this to spiral out of control. Can you promise me that?"

"Yes," she answered quickly. "I won't tell anyone."

"Good." His hand squeezed hers lightly before pulling away. "And if anything else happens, come straight to me."

"I will," she promised. "Thank you, Peter…for helping me through this mess."

As she stepped outside his cottage, the sky overhead stretched endlessly, a sea of stars pulsing like beacons of quiet reassurance. For the first time all night, the fear that had gripped her began to loosen. She inhaled slowly, letting the beauty of the celestial display melt away the rest of the stress.

A quiet sense of pride stirred within her—for standing up for the voiceless animals who couldn't fight for themselves, and for not giving up on her friend, whom she believed was worth saving.

For that brief moment, the evening felt peaceful. Safe.

But her tenuous calm shattered the second she stepped into her dormitory. Gone were the usual lively chatter and bursts of laughter that made the space feel warm and familiar. In its place was a tension so thick it seemed to vibrate off the walls.

Claire scanned the room, her frown deepening as her gaze settled on Rachel, who sat stiffly on her bed, staring blankly at her laptop. She looked like someone who had just received bad news.

"Rachel?" she ventured cautiously. "What's going on? Why is everyone so…on edge?"

Rachel spun around with a dramatic sigh, snapping the laptop shut. "Looks like the satellite dish is down, broken or something. No internet, no cell service!"

"What? It was working fifteen minutes ago!"

She yanked out her phone, her fingers squeezing it as she stared at the screen. Three words glared back at her: No Internet Connection.

"I know, right? And get this. Someone said it might take

days, *or even a week,* to fix it! Can you imagine?" Rachel threw up her hands in frustration.

Claire's stomach dropped. "That means…we're completely cut off."

Rachel shrugged, trying to mask her irritation with an optimistic grin. "I guess it's not all bad. I mean, we can always play board games, right? Honestly, I'm more upset that I can't call my parents tonight."

"Yeah," Claire murmured, trying to downplay her growing apprehension. "I guess it's not the end of the world."

Rachel flopped onto her bed, throwing herself back against her pillows. "At least you weren't stuck eating alone. Where did you go, anyway? You just bolted out of there!"

Claire hated lying to Rachel, it made her heart ache with guilt, but the truth felt too dangerous to share. *You promised Peter,* she reminded herself.

"Oh, nowhere really," she stammered. "I just…wasn't feeling great. I lost my appetite."

Rachel's silence spoke volumes, but being a sympathetic friend, she chose not to pry any further. Instead, they both made a weak attempt at focusing on their homework, but without the internet, they eventually gave up.

One by one, the rest of the girls followed suit, and the room descended into quiet darkness as the lights clicked off.

But Claire lay awake, staring at the ceiling. The timing of the satellite dish failure bothered her—it happened an hour after she had taken that photograph.

Could someone have purposely damaged it?

When sleep finally came, it brought her no comfort, only a plunge into a realm of nightmares. She was running. The black forest closed in around her, branches snagging at her skin like grasping fingers. Her breathing came in ragged gasps, her legs burned with effort, but the figure behind her was gaining. A guttural cackle slithered through the trees. She risked a glance over her shoulder. It was the third man from the photo, his face contorted in shadowed menace.

He was coming for her...she could feel him closing in, just behind her.

Claire jolted awake with a strangled cry, her chest heaving as if she'd been running for her life. Her hands trembled as she clutched the edge of her blanket, but the nightmare would not let go. The man's sinister laugh continued to ring in her ears.

I need air.

Throwing off the covers, she slipped out of bed and quietly stepped outside, drawn to the cool comfort of the night air. The moon hung high above her, washing the campus in a pale, silvery glow. She took several deep breaths. Slowly, her nerves began to settle. *It was just a dream.*

Then a faint sound reached her ears. A slow crunch of gravel underfoot.

Her head snapped toward the sound. An icy chill coursed down her spine as the hairs on the back of her neck bristled. A figure emerged, detaching itself from the shadows like a specter.

She stumbled backward toward the safety of her dorm, but before she could react further, the figure closed the distance with alarming speed.

A rough hand clamped down over her mouth, cutting off her scream before it could form. Her muffled cry dissolved into a whimper as a pungent, chemical stench filled her nostrils. She thrashed, kicking wildly, but her movements were sluggish, uncoordinated. A heaviness coiled around her limbs, numbing her strength.

Her vision blurred.

The world tilted.

The last thing she felt was the cold crush of fear before she plunged into utter darkness.

Chapter 16

Cold-Hearted Kidnappers

Gradually, the hazy veil of oblivion began to lift as Claire slowly drifted back into consciousness. The first sound to pierce her foggy mind was the faint crackling of fire. Each sharp snap and pop seemed to penetrate her disorientation, pulling her further into awareness.

What happened?

Fragments of memory surfaced—the quiet dorm room, the nightmare that had driven her outside, the search for solace beneath the stars.

And then—

A hand. Smothering. Clamping over her mouth. The smell of chemicals. After that, only blackness.

A violent tremor shook her as the horrifying realization hit. She'd been drugged and kidnapped!

Her limbs felt unresponsive, her thoughts sluggish. She had to shake it off.

Wake up, Claire! Focus!

With great effort, she forced her heavy eyelids open. Immediately, stinging smoke filled her nostrils, making her cough. The air felt thick, suffocating. She blinked rapidly through the haze, her vision sharpening little by little.

She was able to make out a small fire crackling in the center of an empty hut, its flickering light casting sinister shadows across the rough walls. The only exit was a doorway obscured by a thick, filthy blanket, with faint slivers of moonlight slipping through the edges.

A dull ache settled over her body, and a shudder rippled through her. She realized she was lying barefoot on a hard, unforgiving floor, a chill seeping through her thin pajamas.

She tried to move, only to be met with resistance. Her arms were bound tightly behind her back. A jolt of terror crashed into her.

No, no, no.

She fought against the restraints, but they only bit deeper into her wrists. She was trapped.

Suddenly, the blanket over the doorway parted.

Clare stiffened as two figures stepped inside. The first man was tall and muscular, his expression void of emotion as he grabbed her by the arm and hauled her upright. Pain shot through her shoulders, but she barely registered it.

Her eyes were locked on the second man. The gray beard. The cold, penetrating eyes. The carved-from-stone features. It was the man from the photo!

A gasp escaped her throat before she could stop it—betraying her recognition.

"What's your name?" he demanded.

Her throat went dry. "What's g-going on? Why am I here?"

The man's face contorted in irritation. "I'm the one asking the questions. What. Is. Your. Name?"

"Claire," she sputtered. "Claire Thompson."

His cruel gaze bore into her. "I saw you on campus tonight. You took a picture of us. What did you do after that?"

Claire's breath hitched. A tight knot twisted in her stomach. "I didn't take…"

His eyes narrowed. "Don't even try to deny it. We know you did. Now, what did you do after that?

"I…I uploaded it to…to m-my computer," she stammered.

His expression remained unchangeable. "Yes, I know that. *Who* did you tell about it?"

He leaned in closer, his breath stale with tobacco. "And

don't even think about lying. We've been watching you all night."

Her mind scrambled for an answer. *Think, Claire. Say something.*

"I...I might have mentioned it...to Professor Miller." The words tumbled out before she could stop them. Instantly regretting involving Peter, she quickly added, "But he didn't think it was important. He told me to forget it."

A long, tense silence stretched between them.

Then, the accomplice gripping her arm let out a cold, humorless laugh. "She's telling the truth," he declared. "I followed her to Miller's place. After she left, I took care of the satellite dish. Had to be quick about it. Now, no signal, no internet. Nothing." The man smirked. "And while she was out cold, I took a little trip inside her dorm. Didn't wake a soul, which was lucky...for them."

Please, God, no...

"Her phone and laptop?" he announced, relishing the moment as he delivered the final blow. "Both taken care of. Permanently."

Her body went rigid as the revelation sank in. *How far are they willing to go to bury the truth?*

The bearded man watched her, amusement glinting in his eyes. "Very good. You didn't lie." Then he leaned in again, his voice like a blade against her skin. "Now tell me this. Did you make a copy? Or show it to anyone else?"

Claire understood the stakes. But her instincts told her to lie about the flash drive, to protect it at all costs.

"N-no," she stammered, her voice quivering as she forced herself to hold his gaze. "There wasn't time. I w-went straight to Professor Miller."

He studied her, searching for any cracks in her story. Finally, he grunted. "For your sake, I hope you're telling the truth."

Then his lips curled into a sinister smirk. "I don't like people coming between me and my money. That kid was about to hand over a boatload of cash for that elephant tusk until you stuck your nose where it didn't belong. Now everything's on hold until we decide what to do next."

"Please," she begged. "Don't hurt him! He's just a student!"

The bearded man laughed. "Oh, sweetheart. Do you think he's so innocent? That kid practically begged us for one of our *special* items. Went looking for us, asked around until he found us. Nah. He's just another greedy snake in the grass, like the rest of 'em."

"That's not true!" she screamed.

But even as the words left her mouth, the truth stood before her, undeniable. She had risked everything for Daniel, convinced he was desperate, that he had been coerced.

But now she saw it clearly—he wasn't a victim at all.

He was a willing accomplice.

The bearded man scoffed at her outburst and strode out of the door. Then, from somewhere outside, low voices drifted through the night. Claire forced herself to listen, straining past the deafening roar of her own heartbeat.

She heard two voices—then a chilling realization struck her. There was a third kidnapper.

Suddenly, one phrase sliced through the air: "It's time we make her disappear."

Disappear? The icy grip of terror tightened around her again.

Moments later, the man returned, his voice carrying a lethal finality. "The boss says we're done with her. Should we finish her off here or let the creatures have some fun?"

Claire's composure shattered. "Please!" she choked out, tears stinging her eyes. "I swear I won't say anything! I just want to go home!"

The man let out a low, cruel laugh. "You think this is some schoolyard scam?" he sneered. "We've got a multi-million dollar business here, and you…" His gaze raked over her with utter disdain. "You are nothing but a gnat buzzing around our operation."

Turning to his companion, he said, "Let the animals take care of her." His voice was calm, almost bored. "Nice and clean."

Then, without another word, he vanished through the opening, not even sparing her a second glance.

Claire's blood turned cold. *Animals? What animals?*

Chapter 17

Breaking the Chains

Before Claire could fully process the horror of his words, a pair of rough hands wrenched her up. His accomplice slung her over his shoulder with sickening ease, her body as weightless to him as a sack of grain.

"No! Please!" Her scream tore through the stillness, only to be swallowed by the vast, indifferent wilderness.

He shoved her into the back of a waiting truck. She slammed against the metal floor, pain exploding in her ribs. Bound and helpless, she struggled against her restraints, but it was useless. She was powerless.

The engine roared to life, and the truck lurched forward. She could barely breathe as they sped through the night, each sharp turn sending her flying, each bruise a testament to her helplessness.

Soon, the grim reality of her situation sank in. She had risked everything in her pursuit of the truth, and now the consequences of that choice bore down on her with an ominous finality.

I should have been smarter. More careful.

A sudden, unbearable image flashed through her mind—her parents back home.

Her mother lay crumpled on the living room couch, her body racked with sobs. Her father paced furiously, demanding answers that never came. One more heartbreak in a family already shattered by loss.

A sob rose in her throat as she pictured them.

Out of nowhere, Rachel's voice drifted through the chaos, a memory from Narok. "God will be waiting for you…once you realize He never left."

The words echoed in her mind. *Is it true? Is God really waiting for me?* The thought stirred a fragile, desperate hope within her.

"God, are you still there?" The words were barely audible over the truck's rumble. "Please save me! I can't do this alone. I'm…I'm not strong enough."

Her voice cracked as tears streamed down her cheeks, soaking into her dirt-streaked skin. "I'm sorry I shut you out. I was just so angry…that you took Tyler away from me."

Tyler.

His name barely escaped her lips before the sting of his loss struck her. His sweet, freckled face burned into her memory —the way he used to grin even when he was too weak to sit up, the way his hand had clung to hers in those final days.

His death had stolen so much from her family. The cruel injustice of it all had left a gaping wound inside her, one she'd filled with bitterness, anger, and defiance. Anything but faith. She had spent the last year running, shutting God out, convinced He had abandoned her.

But now, staring death in the face, she couldn't outrun the truth any longer.

All the resentment had poisoned her, festering like an open wound.

I can't carry it anymore.

She longed for God's presence, the certainty that He was near. She missed the unshakable faith she once carried before grief had snuffed it out.

A sob wrenched from her throat as the burden of it all crashed down.

"God, I've been angry at you for so long," she whispered into the darkness. "Please forgive me. I don't understand why

Tyler got sick, why he had to die. Maybe I never will. But I know you loved him through it all. And I know you love me, too."

In that moment, Claire felt a weight lift, as if the chains she'd carried for so long had finally fallen away. She felt God's love fill the hollow spaces of her heart, and in that love, she found forgiveness.

Her voice grew stronger as she continued. "Please Lord, I need you now, more than ever. I'm so scared. Give me the strength and courage to face whatever's coming. Please protect me and bring me through this."

Then a verse surfaced from her memory: *I can do all things through Christ who gives me strength.* She whispered it. Then again, louder. Each repetition calmed her down and quieted her fear.

For the first time since her capture, she felt anchored in the presence of the only One who could save her now.

Suddenly, the truck screeched to a halt. The jarring motion slammed her body against the side.

A few seconds later, the back door swung open with a metallic clang, and a rough hand yanked her out. She stumbled, her legs weak beneath her.

"Please," she whispered, her voice hoarse. "Don't do this."

The man's sneer twisted in the moonlight. Without a word, he hoisted her over his shoulder again. Through the wilderness he trudged, burdened by the weight of his sinister intentions.

Finally, he stopped and tossed her to the ground with casual indifference. Pain flared, and the rough earth pressed against her skin.

"Don't worry," he taunted. "The animals can smell fear a mile away. It won't take long."

He turned, his boots crunching as he disappeared into the night. Moments later, the distant rumble of the truck faded into silence.

Claire lay sprawled on the cold earth, the man's parting words echoing in her mind. The cruel irony wasn't lost on her.

After swearing never to put herself at the mercy of the wild again, she had been thrown straight into its jaws.

She curled her body up against the chill, her chest rising and falling in quick, uneven rhythms.

She was alone. Abandoned. Hunted.

Fear whispered that she was helpless, that this was the end. But deep within, beyond the terror and exhaustion, a certainty began to stir—one that pushed back against her fear.

She was *not* alone.

God was here, just as He had been all along. And that truth, that unwavering presence, ignited something fierce inside her.

A spark. A fight.

I will NOT be prey tonight. The vow rang through her like a war cry.

With a deep breath, Claire braced herself for the fight of her life.

Chapter 18

Into the Shadow of Death

With a groan, Claire forced herself upright, every muscle shrieking in protest. Her legs buckled, threatening to give way. She squinted into the darkness.

A road. There has to be a road nearby.

But her surroundings felt like an infinite void. The tall grass whispered with unseen dangers, as the night closed in around her. Pain throbbed in her wrists, the rope biting deep into her skin. Yet, a spark of defiance still burned within her. She stumbled forward into the unknown.

Above her, the African sky glittered with stars, and the full moon cast a soft glow over the terrain, lighting her way. It felt like a sign from above—a quiet promise that God was there.

But as she pressed forward, the wilderness fought back. Jagged rocks bit into her bare feet, and a thorn-laced bush snagged her flimsy pajamas, leaving stinging cuts on her skin. Every step was a battle, but she refused to stop.

"Please, God, give me strength," she whispered into the darkness.

It wasn't long before the endless landscape blurred her sense of time and direction. Was she moving toward the road or deeper into the wilderness? The uncertainty chipped away at her resolve.

Suddenly—a sound. A low, guttural growl.

She froze.

Another growl echoed. Closer this time—deeper and more threatening.

There was no time to waste; she had to find a way to break free from her restraints. Then, as if sparked by divine inspiration, an idea came to her. The thorn bush!

She quickly retraced her steps. If she had any chance of survival, she had to find that bush. Her eyes frantically searched the shadows until she spotted it.

Dropping to her knees, she pressed the ropes against the jagged thorns. Gritting her teeth, she began to saw, each movement sending searing pain through her skin. She could feel her fingers becoming slick with blood but she didn't stop. She couldn't.

Finally, with a satisfying snap, the last strand of rope gave way. She tore the bindings from her wrists and flung them away. Every nerve was on edge, her senses heightened as she scanned the night, straining to catch any sign of movement.

Then she saw them.

A pair of glowing eyes materialized—low to the ground, watching. Then another. And another. Six pairs in total.

Her stomach clenched as the creatures slunk into view, their movements silent, predatory. Hyenas.

Run!

She tore through the darkness, her heartbeat a relentless drum in her ears. The ground blurred beneath her as she pushed her body beyond its limits, muscles screaming, lungs burning with each breath.

The snarls grew louder. The pounding of paws closed in.

"Please, Jesus, help me!" she cried, her voice raw with desperation.

Just as her legs threatened to give out, a lone acacia tree loomed in the darkness. A memory flashed—the lifeless gazelle from her excursion, hoisted into a tree to keep it safe from scavengers…like hyenas. This was her only chance.

Claire sprinted toward it and leapt for the lowest branch, but her blood-soaked fingers slipped against the rough bark. She frantically scrambled up the trunk, then with a final desperate heave, she hauled herself up to a branch just as a hyena lunged, his razor-sharp teeth snapping inches from her dangling foot.

She climbed higher until she found a narrow perch fifteen feet above the ground. Below her, the animals prowled, their eerie laughter echoing through the stillness.

Her nightmare from earlier came rushing back—the race through the darkened forest, the man's chilling cackle as he chased her, the overwhelming terror of it all.

But this time, it wasn't a dream. It was real. She was trapped inside her own nightmare.

Throughout the night, she clung to the tree, her body pressed tightly against the rough bark, the cold night air biting at her skin. Her muscles quivered with exhaustion, each tremor a reminder of the hours she had spent fighting to stay awake and hold on.

As dawn broke, the orange sky chased away the shadows —and, with them, some of her fear. She knew that predators retreated with the light, and for the first time in hours, she allowed herself a fragile sense of hope.

But as the sun climbed higher, her hope began to wither —the hyenas remained, their hunger keeping them anchored to the tree.

After hours under the merciless sun, dehydration sapped the last of her strength. Her throat blazed like fire, and her limbs felt heavy and sluggish. For the first time since climbing the tree, she closed her eyes.

I can't do this anymore.

And then, like a whisper in her soul, a quiet reminder broke through the despair.

God has brought me this far. He will not abandon me now.

All of a sudden, the hyenas, once lethargic in the heat, began to stir. Claire followed their gaze and spotted a Maasai youth draped in a red blanket, his herd of goats trailing behind him.

"Hey!" she called, her voice hoarse and weak. She tried

again, louder. "Help! Please!"

The boy's head snapped toward her, his eyes widening in fear as he spotted the hyenas prowling under the tree. For a brief second, he hesitated, his body tensed with uncertainty. Then, he spun around and bolted, his goats scattering in a flurry of dust as they followed him.

"No!" she screamed, her voice cracking. "Wait! Please don't leave me!"

Her hope for rescue vanished as she watched him disappear into the shimmering horizon.

A deep ache settled into her body. Maybe surrendering would be easier.

Her thoughts drifted to her Savior. "Lord," she whispered, "thank You for never leaving me." A bittersweet comfort settled over her, the thought of reuniting with her brother softening the edges of her fear.

This is how it'll end.

Then she heard a distant sound. A beating rhythm, deep and steady, growing louder.

Through the haze of heat, she saw figures emerge on the horizon. Tall. Strong. Moving with purpose.

Maasai warriors.

"Up here," she croaked, her voice barely more than a whisper.

They approached the tree cautiously, spears in hand, clubs at the ready. The hyenas snarled in defiance, standing their ground, their eyes flashing with hunger.

One beast lunged—jaws snapping, but a warrior met the charge head-on, his spear plunging with lethal precision. The creature crumpled to the earth, blood pooling from the wound.

The remaining pack, sensing defeat, slinked away into the savanna, their eerie laughter fading into the distance.

A broken sob escaped her lips. *I'm saved.*

But her relief came too late. Her strength evaporated in an instant, and her body collapsed under the weight of exhaustion.

She let go of the branch.

The world spun around her, a blur of motion, and then the hard ground rushed up to meet her in a brutal embrace.

Chapter 19

Healing Hands

Hovering at the edge of consciousness, Claire felt herself being lifted—weightless, adrift. Then an intense, searing pain tore through her arm and shoulder, forcing a strangled cry from her parched lips. Then, everything went black.

Acrid smoke curled into her nostrils, yanking her back to consciousness. Her eyelids fluttered, heavy with exhaustion, reluctant to open. The biting cold of the earth was gone. Beneath her was something softer—a thin, lumpy mattress.

She cracked her eyes open. Shadows from a small fire flickered over the rough walls of a native hut, stretching and twisting into eerie shapes that clawed at the edges of her memory.

"I'm back in the poacher's hideout!" she choked out, her voice raw with panic.

She scanned the room quickly, but something felt... different.

Instead of emptiness and decay, the space appeared lived-in. Blankets were carefully arranged on crude beds, and a wooden shelf held an assortment of cooking tools. The air carried the warm, herbal scent of something medicinal.

Slowly, reason took hold as she realized it could not be the same place. The stiffness in her chest loosened, and her breath began to steady.

She tried to sit up, but a wave of dizziness forced her back down. Through the spinning haze, a woman emerged, draped in vibrant Maasai attire, her dark eyes filled with something Claire hadn't seen in a long time.

Compassion.

The woman knelt beside her, dipping a wooden spoon into a bowl of liquid and gingerly bringing it to her lips.

"Kunywa," she offered in a low tone, coaxing her to drink.

Claire hesitated, fear still whispering at the edges of her mind. But the woman's patience, her quiet kindness, chipped away at her reservations. Finally, she parted her lips, letting the warm liquid trickle in. It was bitter, but soothing, easing the rawness in her throat.

The woman began to carefully tend to Claire's wounds, applying a white salve over her wrists and wrapping her battered feet in clean bandages. As the soothing coolness touched her skin, her mind drifted back to her barefoot sprint through the bush—each step a fresh stab of pain.

Yet, despite the haunting memory, gratitude swelled within her, like a tide rising to wash away her fear. *God saved me. He delivered me from my nightmare and brought me here.*

"Thank you," she whispered, hoping she understood the sincerity in her voice.

The woman smiled, responding smoothly in her own language. Claire didn't understand, but the gentleness in her expression spoke louder than words.

Before long, her eyelids grew heavy, and she surrendered to sleep once more.

∞∞∞

Claire blinked awake, disoriented by the shift from darkness to light as soft daylight filtered through the woven doorway. Time felt like a forgotten melody, its rhythm lost in the haziness of sleep. Beside her, the same Maasai woman sat silently, keeping a watchful vigil.

"How long have I been here?" Claire asked softly. She didn't expect an answer, but the question escaped anyway.

The woman simply smiled.

Claire shifted, attempting to sit up, but when she moved, an excruciating pain shot through her left arm. She gasped, collapsing back onto the mattress.

Then she saw it.

Her elbow was swollen, deep bruises darkening it to a sickly purple. Bent at an unnatural angle, it sent a wave of nausea through her. Her fingers tingled, numb from lack of circulation.

The woman pointed to her injured limb. "Mbaya."

Claire didn't need a translation. Her arm was badly broken, too injured for simple bandages and herbal salves.

The throbbing made her head spin and her vision blur, and as she slipped into oblivion again, a desperate plea formed in her mind.

Please, God, don't let me die here.

∞∞∞

The next day the Maasai woman carefully secured a crude splint around Claire's arm and shoulder. But despite her efforts, the relentless throbbing refused to subside.

The woman stayed by her side, giving her medicinal tea, rewrapping the bandages, and offering what comfort she could.

By the third morning, the truth became clear to Claire: she needed real medical help.

She was still turning this over in her mind when the doorway darkened. Several Maasai warriors stood at the entrance, their imposing silhouettes filling the space as the morning light cast shadows across their faces. They spoke in hushed tones, their words low and unfamiliar.

Forcing herself to stay calm, she asked, "Do any of you speak English?"

Silence.

She gestured to her broken arm. "It needs more care."

The men observed her, expressions impossible to read. After a brief exchange, they strode out of the hut.

A sinking feeling took hold as she watched them disappear.

Are they going to help me? Or are they going to leave me here?

Minutes crawled by, each one stretching her nerves tighter. Then hours.

Just as despair began to settle in, a sound pierced the silence—the steady rhythm of footsteps.

Not the heavy march of multiple warriors returning. Just one.

Someone was coming.

Chapter 20

The Missionary

As the entrance flap rustled, a terrifying image flooded her mind—the bearded man seizing her, pulling her into the shadows, and plunging her back into the nightmare.

She held her breath, a thick knot of fear closing off her throat.

But instead of the kidnappers, a young man stepped inside, his movements slow, deliberate—as if he were gauging her reaction, assessing the situation.

In the dim glow of the fire, she could make out his features. Mid-twenties. Wavy blond hair curling out from beneath a tan safari hat. His sun-kissed skin suggested he spent most of his time outdoors, but it was his eyes—warm, brown, yet sharp—that held her attention. They scanned her splinted arm, concern flickering in their depths.

"Hello," he said, his American accent jarring against the unfamiliar language she had been hearing. "I'm John McKenzie, but most folks call me Jack." He offered a small, reassuring smile as he sat down on the bed next to her. "I'm here to help you."

Claire went rigid, pulling the blanket tighter around herself as she studied him suspiciously.

When she didn't respond, he continued, his tone patient. "The village chief sent one of his men to my orphanage this morning to fetch me. I'm a missionary there," he explained. "He told me they found a woman alone in the wilderness who needed medical attention. So…here I am."

She studied him, searching for any sign of deception. His expression seemed to be open and sincere, but so had Daniel's. The memory of that betrayal twisted like a knife in her gut.

Feeling the need to test him, she asked, "If you really *are* a missionary, then what's your favorite Bible verse?"

Jack's mouth curved into a small grin as he reached into his bag and pulled out a worn, leather-bound Bible. "Fair question." Flipping through the pages, he stopped at a familiar passage.

"How about this one: 'I can do all things through Christ—'"

"Who gives me strength," Claire finished softly.

Jack laughed lightly, his expression warm. "Looks like we have something in common. That verse has carried me through a lot. I'm guessing it's done the same for you."

Instantly, she was back in the wilderness, clinging to that verse like a lifeline. Now, hearing it spoken aloud, the dam she had carefully built around her emotions began to crack.

Tears spilled down her cheeks, her body trembling with sobs as the weight of everything she had endured came crashing down on her.

Jack didn't speak, didn't rush her. He simply waited, allowing her to release what she had held in for so long.

Once she had finished, his words were calm and soothing. "I know you're afraid, but you're safe now. I promise I'll get you the care you need. But can you tell me what happened to you?"

Claire held back for just a moment. After everything she'd been through, trust wasn't something she could afford to give freely. But there was something about him, a confidence and a kindness, that quieted her doubts.

With a quivering voice, she recounted her ordeal. Jack listened without interrupting, his expression filled with patient understanding and concern.

"That must have been horrific, Claire," he responded once she finished her story. "Poachers are known to be merciless. The fact that you survived…honestly, it's nothing short of a miracle."

"It *was* a miracle," she agreed. "I know God saved me." But then, a new fear surfaced. "But now, I don't know what to do. If those men find out I'm alive, I'm sure they'll come for me."

Jack's face grew serious. "You're right. Going to the hospital might not be the best plan. I think the best option is to bring you to my orphanage. It's remote, and I know a missionary doctor who can treat you. You'll be safer there."

She knew accepting his offer meant placing her life in the hands of a stranger. But the warriors had trusted him enough to seek him out. *Maybe, I should, too.*

She nodded. "Okay. I'll go with you."

Jack's face lit up. "Good! My motorcycle's parked outside."

Her eyes widened in alarm. "A motorcycle?"

Her mind immediately conjured an image—barefoot, her torn pajamas flapping in the wind, and her broken arm jostling painfully with every bump as she clung desperately to the back of the bike.

She groaned. "You've got to be kidding me. I can't possibly ride like this!"

Jack smiled patiently. "Claire, I get it. It's not ideal, but it's our best option. The women here can find you something else to wear. And I promise, I'll drive carefully. The nickname 'Crash' was just a one-time thing."

Despite herself, she let out a weak laugh. "That's not reassuring."

The Maasai woman soon returned with a faded dress and a pair of mismatched shoes that were a size too big. She gratefully exchanged her torn pajamas for something more practical.

Jack knelt beside her, attentively adjusting and securing the splint. His quiet focus and gentle touch melted away the last of her resistance.

As she stepped outside the hut, the entire village had gathered to see her off. The Maasai woman who had cared for her stood nearby, her eyes shimmering with unshed tears. Claire wrapped her in a one-armed embrace.

"Thank you," she whispered. The woman said nothing but

tenderly rested her hand on Claire's cheek. The affection in that simple gesture spoke louder than words.

Claire looked at the warriors, offering them a small, grateful nod.

They saved my life, she thought, her heart clenching. *It's a debt I could never repay.*

Moments later, she climbed onto the back of Jack's motorcycle, her good arm wrapped securely around his waist.

The engine rumbled beneath her as they sped across the rugged terrain, the village shrinking behind them. The wind whipped against her skin, tangling her hair, while each bump sent fresh spikes of pain through her battered body.

Despite the throbbing, she was grateful to have escaped the nightmare of captivity and was on her way to someplace safe, where proper medical care awaited.

But soon her relief was overshadowed by a whisper of warning that clawed itself into her thoughts. She wasn't sure if she was heading toward safety—or walking straight into something far worse.

Chapter 21

The House of Hope

The late afternoon sun bathed the orphanage in a golden haze as Jack and Claire pulled up to the gate. A hand-painted sign read House of Hope, with a smaller Jan's scrawled above it, almost as an afterthought.

Claire's broken arm pulsed with pain, while her good arm, stiff and shaky from an hour of clinging to Jack, provided little support. Every jolt of the rugged terrain had drained what little strength she had left.

But as she lifted her weary gaze to the gate, a thought stirred beneath the exhaustion.

Refuge. At last.

Jack slowed the vehicle and gestured toward a cement block building just beyond the gate. "It's not fancy, but it's home for a lot of kids who didn't have one before."

Claire took in her new surroundings. The building was unassuming in its practical, sturdy design, but something about it radiated warmth. Wide stairs led to a long porch spanning the structure's length, and blue, weather-worn shutters framed the window with a homey touch. Dirt pathways wound between smaller outbuildings, and in the distance, a patch of green hinted at a garden. Nearby, a few cows grazed lazily, completing the peaceful simplicity of the scene.

"It feels like…a safe place," she murmured, more to herself than to Jack.

He glanced at her, catching the quiet emotion in her words. "It is. You'll see."

As they climbed the stairs, Jack's gaze fell to Claire's unsteady steps. "You okay?"

She winced. "Just my feet. I guess they're still healing."

Without a second thought, he slipped an arm around her waist, gripping her firmly. She leaned into him, grateful for the support as they moved forward.

Inside, a modest living area unfolded—a mismatched assortment of plastic chairs and threadbare couches arranged in a way that felt casual yet inviting.

"It's so quiet," Claire murmured.

"Most of the children are in school," Jack said softly. "A few are napping."

Across the space, long wooden tables had been pushed together to form a communal dining room, and the air carried a faint, comforting aroma of something savory simmering nearby.

He led her down a narrow hallway, guiding her to the last door. "It's not much," he declared as he pushed it open, "but I hope it'll be comfortable for you."

Claire stepped inside, her gaze drifting over the modest space—a twin bed with a red plaid blanket, a small wooden dresser, and a curtained window overlooking the garden outside.

She exhaled, the weight of the past few days loosening ever so slightly. The uncertainty that had gripped her on the way here no longer felt so suffocating.

"It's perfect."

"Good. Now, try to get some rest. You've been through a lot today. I'll come get you when dinner is ready."

Jack turned to leave, but before she could stop herself, Claire called after him. "Jack?"

He paused, glancing back.

"Thank you."

His smile was warm. "Anytime."

With quiet care, he pulled the door shut behind him.

Soon, exhaustion swept over her, and when sleep came, no shadows chased her, no echoes of danger pulled her under—just rest, deep and unbroken.

∞∞∞

A few hours later, a gentle tap on the door roused her.

"Come in," she murmured, blinking sleep from her eyes as the door creaked open.

Jack peeked inside. "It's time for dinner. While you were resting, I contacted a local missionary doctor. He'll be here tomorrow morning to take a look at your arm."

"That's good to hear." She pushed back the blanket and swung her legs over the side of the bed. Although her arm still throbbed beneath the splint, the promise of a hot meal and real medical care filled her with a quiet expectation, easing the ache.

She followed Jack down the hall, and as they entered the dining area, the scene before her buzzed with warmth and life.

A group of women moved in effortless harmony, their conversation a gentle hum as they set the long table with bowls, cups, and spoons. The faint clinking of dishes blended with the joyful chaos spilling in from the front room.

Children darted around the furniture, their laughter ringing through the space like a melody of pure, unrestrained joy. A handful of toddlers crawled across the floor, their tiny hands stretched out for anyone willing to lift them.

Claire paused, absorbing the scene—the energy, the noise, the overflowing happiness.

Suddenly, a shrill whistle cut through the noise.

"Everyone! This is Claire," Jack called out, gesturing in her direction. "She's going to stay with us for a little while. She hurt her arm, so be gentle, okay? No bumping into her!"

A teenage girl with short black hair and a simple, blue dress stepped forward, her smile warm and inviting.

"Hi, I'm Emily. Do you want me to help you find a seat?"

"I'd love that," Claire replied, falling into step behind her.

The soft hum of conversation filled the room as a woman entered through the back door, balancing a large steaming pot in her arms. The rich aroma of warm spices and slow-simmered stew drifted through the air, wrapping Claire in a comfort she hadn't realized she needed. Her stomach twisted with hunger, a quiet, urgent ache.

As the woman ladled portions into bowls, the children watched eagerly, their eyes bright with anticipation.

When Claire's turn came, she accepted the bowl gratefully. Alongside the stew, a piece of pink fruit, speckled with yellow seeds, rested on the edge of the plate.

Jack settled onto the bench beside her. "That's passion fruit. It's a real treat for the children! A farmer donated some this morning."

"Don't you eat fruit often?"

He chuckled. "Oh no. It's a luxury for our budget."

She took a bite, the tangy sweetness bursting on her tongue. Across the table, a young girl grinned as juice dripped down her chin. Watching her delight, Claire realized how much she had taken small moments like these for granted.

Suddenly, the front door banged open, rattling the windows and drawing every eye to the entrance.

A young woman burst inside, her curly brown hair bouncing wildly as she skidded to a stop. Her bright grin could have lit up the entire room.

"Sorry, I'm late!" she hollered. "Hope I didn't miss the good stuff!"

Jack leaned over to Claire, his voice low. "That's Sadie. Another missionary."

Sadie squeezed between two children, her energy as infectious as their giggles. "Ooh, passion fruit!" she gasped, snatching a piece off a plate and popping it into her mouth with a satisfied sigh.

Only then did she notice Claire seated at the end of the

table.

"Well, hey there! Didn't even see you sittin' over there," she exclaimed, her Southern drawl weaving through her words with an easy charm. "I'm Sadie."

"Nice to meet you. I'm Claire."

After dinner, Claire noticed Jack and Sadie huddled in the corner of the kitchen. Their occasional glances toward her left no doubt that she was the subject of their conversation.

Moments later, Sadie rushed over, her bright smile as unwavering as before. "I just wanted to officially welcome you to the House of Hope!"

Then she looked over Claire's worn, threadbare dress, and a thoughtful look crossed her face. "I was thinking, maybe I could lend you some of my clothes?"

Claire's eyes lit up, gratitude breaking through the weariness on her face. "I'd appreciate that so much! You have no idea how much I've wanted to get out of this dress."

Sadie's grin softened. "Well, sugar, I'll fix that right up. I'll grab some clothes and a few other necessities right away. There's also a cold spring on the property out back where you can freshen up."

As the sun dipped toward the horizon, painting the sky in rich crimson, Claire made her way to the spring.

Kneeling beside the crystal-clear pool, she cupped her hands and lifted the cool water to her face. Each splash did more than wash away the dirt and smoky ash from her time in the Maasai hut. It felt like it was rinsing away the weight of everything she had endured.

When she returned to her room, a neatly folded stack of clothes waited for her on the bed. A soft candle flickered beside them, its golden glow casting gentle shadows against the walls.

She ran her fingers over the fabric, the simple act of kindness settling deep in her chest. She had been given shelter, food, safety, and now something as small as clean clothes.

It wasn't just generosity—it was a reminder that this was exactly where she was meant to be. A lump formed in her throat,

but this time, it wasn't fear.
    It was hope.

    .

Chapter 22

Disappointing News

The fragile peace that had cradled her through the night was instantly tested when a sharp jolt of pain yanked her awake. She instinctively pulled her broken arm close to her chest, feeling the heat radiate from where it throbbed. The stiffness had worsened, turning each movement into a struggle.

She tried to stay calm, but a creeping fear settled in her mind.

What if the injury is worse than anyone realizes? What if there's nothing the doctor can do?

When Dr. Tyson finally entered her room an hour later, Claire pushed herself to sit a little taller, determined to mask her growing anxiety. The doctor's white hair framed a face etched with deep lines, each one a testament to years of experience. He set his worn leather medical bag on the table beside her bed.

"Let's take a look," he said, rolling up his sleeves.

He worked with meticulous care, slowly unraveling the layers of bandages wrapped around her injured arm. Claire clenched her teeth as the cool air met her exposed skin, sending a dull, aching throb spiraling up her limb.

Dr. Tyson's touch was feather-light as he examined the injury, his fingertips pressing gently around the swollen, bruised area, assessing the damage.

Then he skillfully rewrapped her arm, securing it into a sturdier sling designed to offer better support. With the same careful precision, he applied a soothing, cool ointment to the healing wounds on her wrists and feet.

The room was silent, broken only by the faint rustling of gauze and the soft scrape of the ointment tin's lid. The quiet seemed to amplify Claire's sense of foreboding.

Finally, Dr. Tyson met her gaze, his eyes steady and compassionate as he delivered the prognosis she had been dreading.

"You must keep your arm completely immobile," he instructed, his voice carrying a quiet authority. "The fracture is quite extensive, so you'll need specialized care, but I believe you can wait until you return to the States. However, I strongly recommend arranging transportation within the next week to ensure proper treatment."

Claire forced herself to nod, his words cutting through her like a knife.

A week. That's all I have left...

Her dream of photographing the Kenyan wilderness, of immersing herself in the vibrant tapestry of African culture, and of completing her semester—had just been ripped away.

Not because of an accident.

Not because of bad luck.

But because of the poachers who had done this to her.

A fire ignited inside her. Heat rose to her cheeks, and her good hand clenched the edge of the blanket, twisting the fabric as she wrestled with her anger.

Those men had destroyed so much, and they deserved every punishment, every consequence for the terror and suffering they had caused. They shouldn't be allowed to walk away after everything they've done.

Jack's voice broke through the firestorm in her mind. "Okay, that's what we'll do, Doc. We'll ride to Nairobi in a week and find Claire a flight home."

Claire blinked, struggling to process his words. Their finality crashed over her like a cold wave, but it couldn't douse the heat still simmering in her thoughts.

Jack walked the doctor to the front door, murmuring a few words before watching him disappear down the dusty road.

When he returned to Claire's room, he hesitated, leaning against the doorframe, his usual easy grin faltering slightly as he studied her.

"You okay?" His voice was gentle, as if afraid to shatter the fragile hold she had on her composure.

Claire released a slow breath, her grip on the blanket finally loosening. "It's just the news. It's disappointing. Everything I had planned is…gone."

Jack's gaze softened. "Yeah. I get that." Then, he straightened, a determined brightness lifting his tone. "Come on. Let me show you around the compound. It'll take your mind off things."

Claire hesitated, then took a deep breath, deciding that the distraction might keep her mind from continuing to spiral. "Okay," she finally said, reaching for his offered arm.

They set off through the property, the morning sun casting long shadows across the grounds. With each step, the tight coil of her indignation slowly began to loosen its grip.

Jack led her past a pen of bleating goats, a thriving garden, and a row of weathered but sturdy outhouses. He pointed to a concrete block building in the distance.

"That's our outdoor kitchen," he stated.

Claire exhaled, letting herself take in the place around her. The orphanage was more than a shelter. It pulsed with life and purpose.

"This place is amazing, Jack," she finally remarked. Then, curiosity nudged at the edge of her thoughts. "But where does the funding come from to run it?"

"Our American sponsor is why we exist," he explained. "She created this place to give orphaned Maasai children a home."

"Is your sponsor's name Jan?" she asked.

His head snapped toward her in surprise. "Yes! How did you know that?"

"I saw the sign on the gate."

"That's right!" he chuckled. "I forgot that Sadie scribbled her name up there ages ago. Jan likes to stay behind the scenes, but we couldn't do this without her."

They ended the tour at the goat pen, where playful baby goats frolicked among the adults. With a quick hop over the fence, Jack scooped up a tiny kid and gently placed it in Claire's good arm.

The little creature let out a loud bleat. Claire startled and then, before she could stop herself, laughter spilled out, bright and unrestrained. As the sound faded, so did the last of her anger.

For a moment, everything felt lighter. The ache of lost dreams and the sting of the doctor's disappointing news—all of it seemed to lift, if only briefly.

She looked over at Jack and caught him staring at her. "What?"

He quickly averted his eyes and stammered, "Nothing. I, uh... like seeing you laugh, that's all."

A gentle warmth bloomed inside her, catching her off guard. As he carefully returned the baby goat to its pen, she swallowed against the strange fluttering in her chest.

She wasn't sure what to do with it.

Or if she even should.

They began to walk back to the orphanage in silence, their steps unhurried, but the space between them hummed with an unspoken energy.

Neither said a word, yet the quiet felt fuller—the kind that whispered of possibilities neither was ready to acknowledge.

Chapter 23

Storms & Sparks

The following days settled into a quiet rhythm, each moment at the orphanage stitching together the tattered edges of her heart.

At first, Claire braced herself for the fear to creep back in—but instead, something else unexpected took its place.

The laughter of children filling the courtyard, the warmth of Sadie's conversation, and the steady presence of Jack, always nearby, softened the hard edges of her thoughts.

She hadn't realized how much she'd been holding her breath until she finally let it out.

The House of Hope was no longer just a refuge.

It had become a sanctuary.

Evening devotions became one of her favorite times for reflection and renewal. The children would gather in the spacious living room, their faces illuminated by the flickering glow of the lantern as Jack offered a brief message of encouragement.

One evening, Claire listened to Jack's devotions centered on 2 Timothy 4:18. His voice was steady as he read to the children:

"The Lord will rescue me from every evil attack and will bring me safely to his heavenly kingdom."

As he finished, his gaze darted toward Claire for the briefest second before he turned back to the children.

"This verse was written by Paul while he was in prison," he explained. "He was facing persecution, punishment, and even death. But instead of despairing, he praised God. Why? Because he was confident in his eternal destiny. He knew that no matter what happened to him, he was already safe in God's hands."

Claire swallowed. *Already safe.* The words whispered through her mind, quiet but insistent.

Jack continued. "And that's the promise we have, too. The Lord will rescue us from every evil. Even when our situation looks hopeless, God is still faithful. We don't have to be afraid. Instead, we can rejoice because He has already won the victory."

As his words filled the room, Claire felt herself being pulled back to the night of her kidnapping. The darkness closing in. The suffocating fear. The overwhelming evil that threatened to consume her.

Then, the sheltering branches of the tree. The Maasai warriors who had come to her rescue.

She had survived.

Not by chance. Not by her own strength.

But by the One who had guided her steps long before she even knew where they were leading.

Later that evening, a rare Kenya thunderstorm rolled in. Rain drummed against the roof, its rhythmic pattern breaking the stillness of the orphanage, while flashes of lightning flickered in the distance. The scent of damp earth mingled with the faint tang of lantern oil in the cool air.

Drawn by the storm, Jack, Sadie, and Claire wandered onto the porch, where the lantern's glow cast flickering patterns across the floor. They eased into their chairs, letting the rain's cadence and the distant rumble of thunder fill the silence, the quiet comfort of shared company settling between them.

After a while, Jack leaned back, his fingers loosely wrapped around a steaming cup of chai. As the rain pattered steadily against the eaves, he shared stories about the orphanage, revealing that, at just twenty-five, he had recently stepped into the role of director after the previous leader fell ill.

"I never imagined I'd end up in this position," he admitted. "But this place has a way of finding its way into your heart."

"You're doing such a fine job, too," Sadie chimed in. "And the kiddos look up to you somethin' fierce."

Jack gave a small, appreciative smile. "Thanks, Sadie. But if you'd arrived before me, you might be the director right now."

Sadie snorted. "Not a chance! I'm a short-term missionary. Two years and I'm back in Georgia to start a whole new chapter of my life!"

Sadie turned to Claire, her eyes gleaming with curiosity. "What about you? What's your big plan after graduation?"

Claire's face brightened. "I've always loved nature photography. I hope to turn it into a career someday. In fact, the pictures I took in the animal reserve a few weeks ago were especially meaningful to me..."

But even as she said it, her thoughts drifted to her camera tucked away in her dorm room. Or at least, she hoped it still was.

Turning to Jack, she hesitated before asking, "My camera means so much to me. Do you think we could stop by my campus to get it before heading to the airport?"

The warmth in Jack's gaze cooled into something cautious. His fingers tensed around his mug. "I'm sorry, Claire. I know how important that camera is to you, and I wish you could get it back. But, it's too dangerous to return to your campus right now. Maybe when things settle down, Sadie and I can look into it. For now, let's focus on keeping you safe."

The thought of losing her camera, and the irreplaceable memories it held, cut deeper than she expected. She instinctively wanted to argue, to push back—but she knew Jack was right. She let out a deep sigh that seemed to echo the rain's gentle rhythm.

Noticing the disappointment on Claire's face, Sadie's expression softened. She sprang to her feet, throwing her arms wide.

"Alright, enough of these long faces. Group hug!"

Claire couldn't help but smile, and Jack's laugh followed, a

soft, unguarded sound that eased the remaining tension.

But when Sadie pulled them both into a warm, slightly squished embrace, his laughter faded. His body stiffened, muscles tensing beneath Claire's touch. The shift was subtle, as if the sudden closeness had pulled him back behind an invisible wall.

Then, slowly, his arm tightened around her. She could feel his warm breath against her hair. For a heartbeat, she let herself lean into it—the rhythmic rise and fall of his chest, the solid presence of him beside her.

After a moment, Claire eased back, but when her eyes met Jack's, something crackled between them. Almost at the same time, they looked away, as if acknowledging it might set something in motion neither of them was ready for.

Jack cleared his throat. "Alright, then. Um, sleep well, everyone."

There was a rough edge in his voice. He hesitated before stepping back, his movements slower, like part of him couldn't quite bring himself to leave.

Claire lingered on the porch for a moment before heading to her room. The connection between her and Jack was undeniable, a current that hummed with possibilities.

But it couldn't last.

In a few days, she would be gone. Back to the States. Back to her old life.

And Jack? He would become just another memory she'd have to leave behind.

Don't get attached to him.

The words echoed like a warning.

But as she stepped into the quiet of her room, the warmth of his touch still lingered on her arm, and an unsettling truth whispered back...

What if I already am?

Chapter 24

Close Call

Jack and Claire were just finishing breakfast when Sadie breezed into the dining room, her bag slung over her shoulder. "I'm headin' into town to pick up the mail." Her voice cut through the soft hush of the morning. "I'm borrowing your motorcycle."

Jack didn't look up from his cup of chai. "Okay."

Sadie gave a casual shrug. "Oh, and I might swing by Claire's campus—catch up with a friend who works there. Maybe I'll do a little pokin' around, and see what's been goin' on."

Jack's mug paused midway to his lips. "Sadie, do you really think that's a good idea? I told you last night—the campus isn't safe."

"Relax, Jack." Sadie waved off his concern with a breezy flick of her hand. "It's not safe for *Claire.* No one can tie me to her—I'm just some random missionary."

A muscle tightened in Jack's jaw. "I don't like it."

Sadie sighed, impatience curling around the edges of the sound. "All I'm gonna do is grab lunch with my friend, chat a bit, and see what I can find out. It's not a big deal. Really."

Silence stretched between them. Finally, the resistance in Jack's expression crumbled. "Okay. Just…be careful."

As Claire listened to the exchange, her thoughts drifted to Rachel. She had tried not to dwell on it, but she was concerned that Rachel was still on campus—surrounded by the same danger Claire had barely escaped. If Sadie was already heading that way, maybe she could finally put her mind at ease.

"Sadie?" Claire asked. "If you do stop by, could you check on my friend Rachel? Just make sure she's okay?"

Sadie's smile was all sunshine and ease. "Of course, sweetie."

But as the hours passed, Claire's certainty slowly began to unravel. *Poking around.* The phrase kept repeating in her mind. What had once seemed like a harmless idea now felt reckless—and maybe a little overconfident.

Jack hadn't said much since Sadie left, but the stress in his posture told her enough. He felt it too.

When Claire stepped into the dining room early in the afternoon, a different kind of tension awaited her. A cluster of children stood near the table, their wide eyes filled with worry.

"What's going on?" Claire asked Emily, one of the older girls, her voice low but urgent.

"It's Grace," she replied, her gaze shifting rapidly. "She doesn't look good."

A cold knot tightened in Claire's stomach. "Show me."

Emily turned and hurried to the girls' dormitory, Claire right behind her.

Grace, a tiny girl no older than six, lay tangled in her thin blankets. Her breathing was shallow, and a sheen of sweat matted her dark curls against her forehead.

Claire knelt beside her, her hand instantly registering the intense heat radiating from the girl's forehead.

"She's burning up." Claire tried to keep her voice calm. She gently shook the girl's small shoulders. "Grace? Can you hear me?"

No response.

Claire swallowed against the rising panic. Turning to Emily, she asked, "When did this start?"

"This morning," Emily said, her voice catching. "She was talking then...but now, she's not."

I need Jack.

Claire bolted down the hall to Jack's door. She pounded on it, her knuckles smarting from the force.

No answer.

She spun around, her gaze locking onto the cluster of children hovering nearby.

"Does anyone know where Mr. McKenzie is?"

Emily shook her head. "I looked everywhere. I couldn't find him."

Then a small boy stepped forward. "The garden, maybe?"

Claire burst through the back door and sprinted toward the garden, her breath coming in quick, shallow bursts.

She found Jack there, crouched among the plants, a basket of ripe tomatoes cradled in his arms.

"Jack!" Her voice rang out with urgency. "It's Grace! She's really sick."

Immediately, the basket slipped from his grasp, tomatoes scattering across the ground as he shot to his feet. "Where is she?"

"In her room," Claire gasped, breathless as she hurried to keep up with him. "She has a high fever...and I couldn't get her to wake up."

Jack dropped to his knees beside the little girl's bed, his fingers pressing against her tiny wrist. When he looked up, his eyes held the answer—her pulse was too weak.

"We need Dr. Tyson," he announced, his voice strained. "He should be at the village clinic."

He jumped to his feet. "I'll leave immediately."

"I'd like to go with—"

"No, Claire," he cut her off, shaking his head. "The motorcycle only holds two, and I need room for the doctor."

Then, suddenly, Jack slammed his fist against the bedpost with a crack that echoed through the room causing Claire to jump.

"Sadie took the motorcycle," he muttered, his frustration boiling over. "I should've planned for this. I should've had a backup." His voice was rough with self-reproach. "I have no choice. I have to run there."

But Claire was already moving. "Then I'm coming, too."

Jack spun to face her. "It's over a mile away. Your feet—"

"I can handle it," she shot back. "I'm a runner, Jack. I can keep up. And an extra set of eyes might help us find the doctor quicker. I *need* to help Grace!"

Only days ago, Claire had been the victim—helpless, powerless.

Not this time. Now, she would act.

Emily stepped forward. "I'll stay with Grace," she said quickly. "The cook will be here soon if we need anything."

Jack hesitated for only a second before nodding. "Okay. Let's go."

They sprinted toward the clinic, the midday sun beating down on them, turning the distance into an unforgiving stretch of heat and dust. Each breath scorched Claire's lungs, but adrenaline pushed her forward.

It didn't take long before every step sent sharp stabs of pain radiating through the scabs on her feet. But she gritted her teeth, determined not to betray her discomfort.

This is temporary. Helping Grace is what matters!

Beside her, Jack stole quick glances her way. Checking. Watching.

Finally, the clinic came into view. Jack reached the door first, knocking—then pounding—against the wood.

"Dr. Tyson!" Jack's urgent voice cut through the stillness. "It's an emergency!"

No answer.

He yanked at the handle. Locked.

Jack's eyes darted around the empty village—no movement, no sign of the doctor.

"Great," he muttered, his voice tight with frustration. "If he's not here, we'll have to find another way."

Claire rested her palm on his back. "We'll find him, Jack."

She raised a hand to shield herself from the harsh glare, her gaze sweeping the horizon. Beyond the huts, a small flicker of movement caught her eye—a woman sat outside, sorting maize, her hands moving in a steady, practiced rhythm.

"Jack," she said, gripping his arm. "Over there!"

They rushed to the woman, and Jack spoke to her in swift, fluent Swahili. She listened intently, then gestured down the dusty road.

Without hesitation, they sprinted ahead, feet kicking up clouds of red dust, the world blurring around them.

At last, a figure appeared—Dr. Tyson, his medical bag swinging in rhythm with his stride.

"Dr. Tyson!" Jack yelled. "We need you at the orphanage. Now!"

A shadow crossed the doctor's face, and he gave a quick nod. He clutched his bag, falling into step with them as they raced back.

By the time they arrived, dusk had already begun to settle over the orphanage. Dr. Tyson was at Grace's side the moment they entered, moving with practiced efficiency. His hands worked quickly, examining the little girl and administering medicine, his calm presence steadying the room.

Claire hovered in the doorway while Jack paced nearby, tension rippling through the air.

Then, at last, Dr. Tyson turned to them. "She's going to be okay."

Jack let out a slow, unsteady breath. The stress that had gripped him slowly drained away. It felt as if the orphanage itself exhaled, the crisis now behind them. All that remained was the soft rustle of blankets and the gentle rhythm of Grace's breathing.

Jack knelt beside the little girl, tucking the blankets around her before gently placing a worn stuffed animal in her small arms.

"Here you go, Gracie," he whispered, his voice soft with reassurance. "Now you're as snug as a bug in a rug."

Claire's heart swelled at his tenderness—the way he cared, the way he protected. The moment reminded her of the Maasai woman's kindness to her when she needed it the most.

After a few minutes, Claire stepped outside and made her way to the porch. She drew in a deep breath of the crisp evening air, but exhaustion swept over her in a sudden, heavy wave. Her knees buckled, and she sank into a chair, her body yielding to the overwhelming feeling of relief.

A moment later, Jack sank onto the chair beside her. His usual confidence seemed to have slipped away, leaving visible weariness in its place. "That was a close call."

Claire nodded. "Your quick action probably saved her life."

Jack's voice was quiet but sincere. "I couldn't have done it without you, Claire. You kept me grounded when I was losing it. And if you hadn't spotted that woman, we'd never have found the doctor in time." He turned to her, a gentle warmth in his eyes. "We make a good team."

In the dim lantern blow, warmth crept into Claire's cheeks. She dropped her gaze, hoping he hadn't noticed. "We do," she murmured, her heart beating a little faster.

A long sigh escaped him as he leaned back in his chair, a faraway look on his face.

Claire studied him closely. The lines on his face were deeper, the set of his shoulders more slumped than she remembered. He looked…worn. Utterly worn.

He gave so much. He poured himself out, day after day.

Why? The question echoed in her mind. *What drives him to do this?*

She paused for a moment, her gaze drifting toward the orphanage before she asked, "Jack, your job is so hard…and it takes so much out of you. Why do you keep doing it?"

A quiet intensity settled over his features. "I know it seems that way, especially on a day like this. But the truth is, I love what I do. I'm from Michigan and I used to work in business, buried in numbers and spreadsheets. It was predictable, but it wasn't fulfilling. I wanted more out of life. So, I took a leap of faith and came here—to serve the people who need it most. Especially the children."

His words carried a quiet conviction, the kind that came from a place of deep purpose.

"That's incredible, Jack," she replied softly, meeting his gaze. "I really admire that." Before she could stop herself, the question slipped out. "Do you have anyone waiting for you back in Michigan?"

He hesitated—just for a second. "No," he answered. "My heart's in Kenya now." His eyes searched hers. "What about you?"

"No," she admitted, the single word feeling both exhilarating and terrifying all at once.

For a moment, neither of them spoke. The quiet evening wrapped around them, as if holding its breath.

Then Jack reached over, his fingers, warm and calloused, slowly curled around hers. The touch was deliberate, tender.

For the first time, she wasn't afraid of the connection. She had spent so much time holding back, uncertain if what they had was fleeting—but now, she knew.

Jack wasn't just someone passing through her life.

He was *meant* to be in it.

His hand lingered, reluctant to part, before he finally let go. The cool evening air slipped between her fingers, a sharp contrast to the warmth he left behind.

The sun dipped lower, brushing the horizon with deep strokes of crimson and amber. Claire peered past the porch into the encroaching darkness, toward the road.

The same road Sadie had taken that morning.

With everything that had happened—the illness, the frantic search for the doctor, and this quiet moment with Jack—Claire hadn't realized how late it had become.

She shifted slightly, her gaze drifting at Jack. "Sadie's been gone all day. I thought she'd be back by now."

Jack followed her eyes to the empty road. "Yeah...but the campus is pretty far away, and you know how she likes to talk." His tone was light, but a shadow of worry crossed his face, gone almost as quickly as it appeared.

Claire nodded, trying to let his words reassure her. But the longer she sat there, the harder it became to ignore the uneasy feeling tightening in her chest.

Sadie should be back by now.

Chapter 25

Sadie's Report

Claire remained on the porch, even after Jack returned inside to help with dinner. Her gaze stayed fixed on the path, her ears straining to catch the distant hum of a motorcycle—any sign of Sadie's return. But as the night deepened and dinner was called, Sadie had not come back.

At the table, each bite turned to dust in her mouth. Her eyes kept darting to the door, her stomach tensing with each passing minute.

By the time the last plate was cleared, Claire's nerves were stretched thin, wound so tight she thought she might snap.

Suddenly, the door flew open.

Sadie burst inside, energy crackling around her like a live wire.

Claire shot to her feet, the pressure in her chest unraveling into a rush of relief.

She's okay.

The worry that had consumed her all evening released its grip, but before she could speak, Sadie was already in motion.

She hastily handed out a few letters, and when she heard about little Grace, she hurried to the girl's room. Bending low, she planted a kiss on her forehead. Grace, already much perkier than before, beamed up at her sleepily.

Finally, as the house settled and the last distractions faded into the soft hum of bedtime, Sadie motioned toward the porch.

Once they were settled, Sadie leaned in, her voice dropping to a conspiratorial whisper. "Okay, I've got some scoop for you. First things first. Rachel's okay."

"Are you sure?" Claire asked.

Sadie nodded. "Yeah. She's shaken but safe. Really worried about you, though. Pretty much everyone on campus is okay."

A weight lifted from Claire's shoulders. "Thank God for that."

Sadie let the relief settle for a moment before continuing. "But the campus has been in an uproar ever since you disappeared. And no one could inform the police right away because the satellite dish was—"

"Sabotaged?" Claire interrupted.

"Exactly!" Sadie exclaimed. "When the police finally got there, they discovered it had been deliberately tampered with. It's fixed now, but they couldn't figure out who did it or why. She dropped her voice lower, the words slipping out like a secret. "But we do, don't we?"

She let the words hang in the air, the truth settling between them.

"And get this—a professor, Miller I think, has been leading search parties every day, questioning everyone. He's like a man on a mission, desperate to find you."

Claire swallowed against the tightness in her throat. *Peter...*

She took a slow breath, forcing herself to focus. "Was there anything else?"

Sadie's expression became more serious. "Unfortunately, yes. I heard that the authorities contacted your parents yesterday. And now they're planning to come to Kenya to join the search!"

Claire's breath caught. Her parents. Here.

The thought barely registered before a sudden suffocating panic crashed over her.

Of course, they would come. If they'd found out she was missing, nothing would stop them. Her mother would be relentless, her father just as determined. They would search, ask questions, push for answers—and walk blindly into the same danger she had only just survived.

"They can't come here!" The words erupted, her fists clenched tight. "It's too dangerous!"

Jack leaned forward, his expression solemn. "If your parents show up at your campus, they'll certainly attract attention, and probably from the wrong people. You're right. It wouldn't be safe for them."

"But with the police involved," Sadie offered, "wouldn't the poachers be lying low?"

Jack shook his head. "There's no guarantee of that. These people are ruthless. If anyone starts poking around their operation, especially outsiders, they'll do whatever it takes to silence them."

Claire gripped the edge of her chair, her knuckles turning white. "I need to warn them!"

Sadie rested a reassuring hand on Claire's shoulder. "We'll figure this out. Maybe you could move your departure up? Get home before they arrive?"

Jack nodded. "That's a good idea. We could leave on Saturday instead of Sunday." He hesitated, as if weighing his words. "And we should stop by the police station before heading to the airport so you can report those men. If they start an investigation right away, it could help protect you and your parents."

"Even if we do, there's no way the police will act fast enough to keep my parents safe!" Claire's voice rose, sharp with urgency. "I need to do something *before* they board that plane."

Sadie sat up straighter. "What if you used Jack's phone to call them? There's no cell service here, but you and Jack could ride out tomorrow morning and try to find a signal. You can tell them what happened but that you're safe—"

"That's risky," Jack cut in, glancing at Claire. "If you tell them too much, they might go straight to the authorities. And if word gets out that you're alive…those men could come after you again."

A heavy silence settled over them, each of them feeling the seriousness of the situation.

Claire exhaled slowly. "I don't have a choice. I have to call them. But I can't tell them the whole truth. I'll just say I'm okay—nothing more."

But doubt curled at the edges of her mind, unraveling her resolve. "But what if they see right through me? I've never been good at lying to them!"

Jack's expression softened. "You'll do great. And if they want to talk to me, I'll be there. We can ride out to a small hill about twenty minutes from here before my medical mission tomorrow. That area usually has the best signal."

Then his face brightened with an idea. "Actually," he said, leaning forward, "why don't you come with me? I'm doing eye checkups in a Maasai village where infections have been a real problem. It'll save me a trip back here after the call, and honestly, I could really use your help."

Her mind flashed to the small boy she had seen in the village outside Maasai Mara—his eyelids swollen, his vision clouded by infection.

Finally, a chance to do something. To help.

A weak smile broke through the anxiety. "I'd love to," she agreed, her words steadier now.

Jack grinned. "Great. So, we'll call your parents first thing tomorrow, then head to the village for the check-ups."

They exchanged a few more words, but exhaustion was pulling at Claire, the weight of the long, emotionally charged day finally catching up with her. She excused herself and trudged back to her room, collapsing into her bed, completely drained.

Lying on her back, eyes fixed on the ceiling, Claire knew that tomorrow she would have to say whatever it took to keep her parents from coming to Kenya—even if it meant lying.

But would it work? Once they made up their minds, they rarely backed down.

I can do this, she told herself, drawing in a slow, steady breath. *I'll just tell them I'm fine.*

But her gaze drifted to the sling cradling her broken arm—a painful reminder of the truth she was hiding.

Nothing about this is fine.

Her pulse quickened, each beat a reminder of how much was at stake.

So much depended on this call. It felt like walking a tightrope over an abyss—one wrong word, one slip up, and everything could come crashing down.

Chapter 26

Bitter Betrayal

Claire lay on the thin mattress, staring at the dim glow of moonlight tracing the cracks in the orphanage ceiling. She tried to hold onto the warmth of Jack's caress from earlier, but sleep still eluded her, her mind consumed by the conversation with her parents that awaited her in the morning.

Anxious thoughts crowded in, and she pressed a hand against her forehead. The room was too warm, too stifling, as if the walls were closing in on her. With a frustrated sigh, she pushed herself upright. Crossing the small room, she moved to the window and nudged it open.

The cool night air rushed in, and she leaned into it, allowing the breeze to unwind the taut coil of tension knotted inside her.

Suddenly, voices drifted from below, piercing the stillness. She stiffened, recognizing them.

Jack and Sadie.

She knew she should close the window, give them privacy. But something in the raw edge of their voices held her rooted to the spot.

Jack's urgent voice cut through. "Please don't cry!" he pleaded. "I'm sorry, Sadie! I didn't mean to hurt you."

Sadie's voice trembled, each word a fragile thread unraveling. "I have to l-leave the orphanage! I c-can't stay here anymore. It's impossible!"

Claire's entire body went rigid. *Leave the orphanage?*

Jack's voice softened but held a desperate edge. "It *is* possible, Sadie. Just don't go! The orphans need you...I need you."

A stab of guilt pierced her. She shouldn't be listening to this. She was trespassing on a moment too raw, too real. But she couldn't move. Couldn't turn away.

What could have happened in the hours since they parted to cause this?

Sadie's voice broke through, splintering the night. "Don't you think I know that, Jack? That's what makes this so hard! But what choice do I have? You said it wouldn't change anything, but we both know that's not true! Our relationship *will* change. Nothing will ever be the same again!"

Relationship?

The word hit Claire like a slap. She gripped the windowsill so tightly, that the rough wood bit into her palms.

Jack's voice dropped to a whisper, so faint that Claire had to strain to hear him. "I'm sorry...I shouldn't have said that. Please forgive me."

"If you...ever cared about me," Sadie choked out between sobs, "you'll let me...go."

A tense silence followed before Jack's voice broke through. "I can't lose you, Sadie."

A rustle followed—soft, intimate. The shift of bodies. Sadie's muffled cries faded, quieting as if pressed against someone's shoulder.

Claire's mind conjured the image—Jack's arms around Sadie, pulling her close.

Her fingers uncurled from the windowsill, and she eased back, lowering the window carefully. The night shut her out, but the hurt had already found its way in.

She stumbled to her bed and sank into it. She pulled the thin blanket around herself, a flimsy barrier against the truth. It wasn't until the taste of salt touched her lips that she realized she was crying.

How foolish she had been. It all seemed so clear now. Jack and Sadie were a couple.

Every lingering glance, every brush of his hand—none of it had meant anything. She had built her hope on an illusion.

When Jack said his heart was in Kenya, she let herself believe he meant *her*. Had she been fooling herself? The quiet moments, the warmth of his hand in hers—had any of it been real?

Her mind flashed back to Daniel—the way he had looked at her, sincerity in his eyes, as he said, 'Just trust me.' And all the while, he'd been working alongside the very poachers she had fought so hard to expose.

She buried her head in the pillow, the fabric muffling the sound of her sobs. It was the same story, retold with new faces. She trusted. She believed—

And was betrayed.

∞∞∞

Sometime between the ragged sobs and the hollow silence that followed, darkness gave way to morning, brushing the world in a dull, unkind light.

Claire hadn't slept. Her eyes burned with grit, and a relentless pounding echoed in her head.

She had spent the night wrestling with the truth that Jack had deceived her and that everything they had shared was nothing more than a mirage of shifting sand.

But now, a sliver of doubt pierced through the haze. She replayed the conversation in her mind—the guilt threading through Jack's voice, the hurt woven in Sadie's words. Something didn't sit right.

A different kind of ache settled over her.

Could Jack have confessed to Sadie that he was starting to develop feelings…for her? Was that the guilt she heard in his voice?

If that was true, then Jack was torn between his growing attraction to her and the bonds that still tied him to Sadie.

But understanding this didn't make the hurt disappear. It only softened the edges of betrayal, dulling the sharpness just enough to let her breathe.

He should have told me, from the very beginning, that he was committed to someone else.

The echo of Sadie's anguished cries pierced Claire's heart, a reminder that, no matter the hurt she felt, she wasn't the only one in pain.

No, she resolved. *I refuse to be the reason Jack and Sadie break apart.*

She sat up, pushing the blanket away.

She had to know. She couldn't let the knowledge of last night's conversation fester into something that might consume her.

She needed to face him—to look into those same eyes that had once brimmed with promise—and demand the truth.

No matter how much it hurt.

Chapter 27

Confrontation

Claire found Jack in the kitchen, his back turned as he worked. Each quiet clink of dishes tightened the knot in her stomach. She drew in a steadying breath, trying to force the tremor from her hands.

When he spun around, his easy, familiar smile nearly undid her.

"Good morning, Claire," he greeted her warmly.

She forced a nod. "Morning."

Jack's smile faded slightly. "Everything okay?"

She shifted her weight, arms folding stiffly across her chest. "Actually, there's something we need to talk about."

His brows drew together. "Okay."

She swallowed, the words sticking in her throat. "I don't think I should go to the Maasai village with you today."

He blinked, caught off guard. "Why?"

A penetrating ache shot through her. "I just…don't think it would be…right."

Jack's frown deepened. "I thought you wanted to go. I could really use your help."

He stepped closer, reaching out—his fingers brushing against hers.

For a moment, she almost gave in. Almost let the warmth of his touch erase the reality of last night. But the memory came crashing back, and she pulled her hand back. She saw the pain flash across Jack's expression before he could hide it.

"I won't be the reason, I mean, I don't want to..." The words tangled on her tongue, cutting into her resolve. She had come for answers, ready to demand the truth, but now, staring into his hurt eyes, her courage began to slip away.

She swallowed the truth. "It's just not a good idea."

"Claire...what's going on?" he pressed.

Ignoring his question, she forced her expression into something unreadable. "When do we leave to call my parents?"

Jack studied her, searching for something she wouldn't give. "I thought we'd leave around ten," he said, his voice quieter now.

She gave him a stiff nod and turned to go, but his voice caught her before she could escape.

"Wait." He stepped closer, just inches from her now. "Something's wrong. Talk to me."

Claire clenched her fists at her sides, fighting the storm building inside her. She had let the chance to confront him slip through her fingers moments ago. But it was too much—the sleepless night, the betrayal, the ache in her heart.

The dam broke, taking her silence with it. She would say what needed to be said. She would get the answers she deserved.

"You want to know what's wrong?" she snapped. "Fine. I know the truth, Jack. You should have told me from the beginning that you and Sadie are together."

A flash of confusion cut across his face. "What?"

"I heard you arguing with her last night," she confessed. "So don't stand here and pretend I don't know what's going on."

He locked his jaw as he set the dish towel down, bracing himself against the counter. "That conversation was private," he finally responded.

"You were right outside my window!" she shot back, her exasperation spilling over.

Jack's eyes narrowed, and a muscle twitched in his jaw. He glanced at the cook nearby, then lowered his voice, his irritation barely contained. "Not here."

He nodded toward the back door. "Come with me."

Before she could respond, he grabbed her wrist, gently but firmly, and tugged her toward the door.

The moment they stepped outside, he released her, running a hand through his hair as if trying to rein in his emotions. "I can't believe this," he muttered.

Claire folded her arms, frustration building as he dodged her question. "Why? Because I figured out what's really going on?"

"No," he snapped. "Because you didn't!"

"Oh, so I just *imagined* everything I heard?"

Jack shook his head. "No, you heard something. But you didn't *understand* it."

Her voice trembled with anger. "It's not complicated, Jack. You've developed feelings for me, told Sadie, and the two of you fought about it. That's the only explanation!"

"No, it's not." He paused, staring at her, a brief moment of tenderness softening his expression. "The only thing you just said that was true is that I have feelings for you."

Her breath hitched in her throat. Even with his confession, she wasn't ready to back down. "Then explain last night," she insisted. "Why did I hear you pleading with her to stay? Why did you tell her you couldn't lose her?"

Jack exhaled slowly, a pained look crossing his face. "I *did* say those things, but—"

"And did you embrace her, Jack?" she cut in, her eyes searching his. "Tell me the truth."

He flinched, as if the question had cut deeper than expected. "Yes, but it wasn't what you think."

She stared at him, disbelief settling in. "Oh? Then what exactly was it?"

His patience eroded, his tone became edgier than before. "An apology. That's all." He paused, softer now, almost pleading. "Claire, I wouldn't show *you* affection if I were with someone else. That's not who I am. I thought you knew that."

Her resolve wavered for just a moment, his sincerity

tugging at her heart. "How am I supposed to trust you after this?"

Jack continued, his voice quiet, as if he were speaking to a version of her that didn't want to hear the truth. "I get that someone lied to you before, but I am *not* that person. And if you can't see that, I don't know what else to say."

Her voice was now a whisper. "Then can you at least tell me what you were arguing about?"

An unspoken battle seemed to play out behind his eyes. "I'm sorry. I...I can't."

A bitter laugh slipped out. "Right. Because keeping me in the dark has worked *so* well!"

For a fleeting moment, hesitation flashed in his gaze—something unspoken, something he couldn't share.

"I don't *want* to keep you in the dark. But sometimes there's no other way."

More secrets. More lies.

"How convenient," she scoffed.

He sighed deeply. "I've told you the truth, but it feels like you've already decided what kind of person I am. I guess you never trusted me at all."

His shoulders slumped, as if the unspoken divide between them now rested heavily on his back. "We'll leave in an hour to call your parents."

There was a cold, detached finality in his tone. Then, without another word, he turned and walked away, leaving Claire standing in the courtyard.

She didn't call after him. Didn't move.

The hurt in Jack's eyes, his final words—crushed her.

She had been so sure that Jack had been hiding his relationship with Sadie from her, so willing to believe that trusting him had been a mistake. But now...his heartfelt denial, the raw honesty in his gaze, shattered her confidence.

Had I let my past fears blind me to the truth? The thought sent a chill through her. *What if I was wrong about it all?*

Now, a different kind of fear took hold.

What she had with Jack wasn't just damaged—it might be beyond repair.

And she wasn't sure even a friendship could survive the fallout.

Chapter 28

Truth Revealed

Claire stood frozen, her thoughts tangled with doubt. The argument with Jack replayed in her mind, and despite her uncertainty, she knew too many pieces of the puzzle were still missing.

Something was going on, and from the sound of Sadie's sobs last night, it was worse than she could have imagined.

Would Sadie tell her the truth?

She had to find her and see if she'd reveal what was really happening. More than anything, she needed to salvage their friendship. The thought of losing Sadie too felt like it might break her.

Claire rushed inside and found Sadie alone in the living room, her eyes dull and distant, the usual spark missing.

She hesitated for a moment before sitting down beside her, her voice tentative. "Sadie, I'm...I'm sorry for whatever you're going through. And if I've made things worse..."

Sadie didn't respond at first, her gaze far away. Then, blinking as though snapping out of a trance, she looked at Claire.

"Wait," she said, her voice unsteady. "Do you think I'm angry with you?"

"I honestly don't know why you're upset," Claire admitted. "I think I have an idea, but I'm not sure."

Sadie exhaled a shaky breath. "I'm just mad about... everything. It's my fiancé Mark." Her voice wavered, barely holding together. "He was just diagnosed with thyroid cancer."

Claire's breath stalled. "Wait...your what?"

Sadie lifted her gaze, her eyes glassy. "Mark...my fiancé," she repeated, her voice softer this time. "I found out yesterday."

It felt as though the floor had vanished beneath Claire's feet. Her voice caught. "Oh, Sadie...that's awful news."

Sadie stared at her hands. "Mark says it's early, but..." She let out a quick breath. "I feel so helpless. I should be there, but he insists I stay. Says this is where I'm needed, that I should finish what I started. But how can I? He's about to fight cancer alone."

Claire swallowed hard, struggling to take it all in. "Did you tell Jack?"

Sadie's fingers twisted in her lap. "Yeah. Last night. He said I should stay at the orphanage. Demanded it, actually. Tried to tell me the cancer wouldn't change my relationship with Mark." She shook her head, blinking back tears. "I was so upset. How could he say that? And I think he felt bad about it because he apologized right after."

The weight of her mistake pressed on Claire like a heavy stone. Jack had tried to explain that she'd misunderstood what she overheard, but she hadn't believed him. She'd refused to see the truth, blinded by her own assumptions.

It had never been about deception...or lies. It had always been about Sadie, caught between duty and love. And Jack, trying to honor the trust she had placed in him.

Claire's mind was still reeling, but then she saw the deep hurt on Sadie's face. She couldn't afford to drown in her guilt. Not when Sadie needed her.

"I understand what you're going through," Claire replied softly. "My brother had cancer, too."

Sadie blinked at her, surprise flickering in her tear-streaked eyes. "Your brother?"

Claire nodded, the hollow emptiness creeping in, settling deep in her heart—the same feeling that always surfaced when she spoke of him.

"Tyler." Claire's voice faltered. "He...he had stage four

colon cancer. By the time they caught it, we only had six months with him."

The familiar ache settled deeper. For so long, she had carried this pain alone, locked it away like a secret, as if keeping it hidden would make it hurt less. But it had only made it worse.

A slow breath.

"But I was there for every second of it." A bittersweet smile tugged at her lips. "And I don't regret a single one."

A tear slipped down Sadie's cheek. "Claire, I...had no idea."

"You weren't supposed to," she admitted. "But I know what it's like to watch someone you love go through this. If I can give you one piece of advice, it's go to Mark." Her voice was firmer now, carrying the weight of experience. "Don't let guilt stop you from being where your heart tells you to be."

Sadie exhaled deeply and nodded, a faint smile forming at the edges of her lips. "Thank you, Claire...for sharing that. I know it wasn't easy." She gave Claire's hand a gentle squeeze before rising to her feet. "I've got a lot to think about."

With that, she excused herself, leaving Claire alone.

For the first time in a long while, speaking about Tyler didn't feel like reopening a wound. It felt like offering a piece of herself that someone else needed. And somehow, seeing the way it had touched Sadie, the way it had *helped*, eased something deep inside her.

Maybe her grief didn't have to be just pain.

But as the warmth of that thought settled, another crept in—the crushing realization that she had been so blinded by old betrayals that she had seen deception where there was none.

She had known what kind of man Jack was, *had seen it with her own eyes,* and still, she had convinced herself otherwise.

And in doing so, she had hurt him. Cut him with words he didn't deserve.

She *had* to fix this.

Claire shot to her feet and tore through the back door.

"Jack!" she shouted. "Jack, I need to—"

Suddenly, a force slammed into her, knocking the breath

from her lungs.

She staggered back, arms flailing for balance—but it was too late.

Her feet flew out from under her, and she crashed to the ground with a heavy thud.

Chapter 29

Forgiveness

Dazed, Claire blinked rapidly, her vision swimming. Sprawled on the hard ground, she gasped for air, her chest rising and falling rapidly. A dull ache pulsed through her broken arm.

Suddenly, a calloused hand grasped her arm. She turned, locking eyes with Jack. He lay beside her, equally breathless, his expression a mixture of shock and concern.

"Jack," she managed to say, pushing herself up on her elbows. "I was looking for you. I just wanted to say that I'm so—"

Before she could finish, Jack quickly closed the space between them. And then, without a word, he wrapped her in a strong embrace.

As his body tightened around hers, the tension that had gripped her for so long melted away. A soft sigh escaped her lips, and she let herself sink into the quiet comfort of his arms.

"Are you alright?" he murmured, his voice rumbling softly against her ear.

Nestled against him, she nodded, his rhythmic breaths calming her racing heart. In that moment, she understood just how deeply she needed him.

Jack eventually pulled back, his eyes scanning her face. "Claire, are you sure you're okay?" he asked gently. "Did you hurt your arm when you fell?"

She flexed her fingers, carefully checking the sling before

shaking her head. "I'm okay," she whispered. "Just a little shaken up."

Then, her emotions surged like a rising tide. Tears welled up, blurring her vision until Jack's features dissolved into a hazy blur.

"I'm so sorry," she blurted out, her words tumbling out in a frantic rush. "For what I said—for accusing you. Sadie just told me about Mark, and I realize now how wrong I was…about you…about everything."

She gasped for air, her voice trembling as she continued. "I convinced myself I couldn't trust you—when all you've ever done is show me how much I can count on you." Her gaze dropped to the ground. "Can you ever forgive me?"

Jack reached up and gently brushed a tear from her cheek. "Claire," he said softly, "it was just a big misunderstanding. Of course, I forgive you. And I'm sorry, too, for losing my temper—I shouldn't have done that."

He tenderly lifted her chin up, making her meet his gaze. "I care for you deeply, Claire, and the last thing I would ever want to do is hurt you."

A weak smile broke through, easing her lingering guilt. "Jack, thank you for that." Then, with a teasing sparkle in her eye, she added, "And just for the record, I'm never eavesdropping again. It's brought me nothing but trouble."

Jack chuckled softly, the tension between them finally lifting. "I'll hold you to that."

Then Jack leaned in slowly, as if drawn by some unseen force—tentative at first, giving her the chance to pull away. But she didn't.

When their lips met, it was soft, unhurried—a kiss that spoke of forgiveness, of understanding, of everything they hadn't been able to put into words.

It wasn't just the end of their argument.

It was the beginning of something new.

Jack's fingers brushed lightly against her cheek as if to tell her *I'm here. I'm not going anywhere.*

And Claire knew—neither was she.

After a moment, they pulled apart, and Jack helped her to her feet.

"Are you still determined to skip the Maasai village?" he asked.

She brushed the dirt from her skirt. "Actually, I was hoping I could still go."

His grin widened. "Of course! That's actually why I was heading back in—to convince you to change your mind." He leaned in slightly, mischief dancing in his expression. "Though I didn't expect knocking you down and kissing you would be the winning strategy."

Her cheeks flushed a rosy hue. "Looks like it worked."

Jack laughed, then clasped his hand in hers. "Come on, let's get going. The motorcycle is fully gassed, and I've packed all the supplies for the medical mission. He paused, giving her hand a light squeeze. "But first…we'll make that call to your parents. Are you ready for this?"

"Not really," she admitted. "But I know I have to do it. They need to be warned."

The ride to the small hilltop was a blur, the rushing landscape mirroring the storm of thoughts swirling in her mind. No matter how hard she tried to steady herself, her fears kept circling back to the same, paralyzing questions—

What if they don't believe me? What if I can't stop them from coming?

When they reached the top of the hill, Jack turned on his phone. There was a signal, weak but there.

He parked and guided her toward a rocky ledge. The open sky stretched endlessly before them, but its beauty did little to calm her nerves.

After a few minutes, he handed her his phone. "You've got this, Claire. I believe in you."

Her fingers curled around the phone. She gave Jack a small nod, inhaled deeply, and dialed.

Each unanswered ring seemed to stretch on forever.

Finally, the call connected.

"Who is this?" The voice on the other end was gruff, suspicious.

The line crackled.

"Dad!" Claire's voice cracked with desperation. "It's me!"

A beat of silence.

His voice returned, edged with caution. "Claire?"

A burst of static filled the line, the signal faltering.

She held her breath.

Please don't drop. Not now!

Chapter 30

Connection

"Claire?" Her father's voice was clearer now. "Sweetheart, is that really you?"

Relief flooded through her, but it was brief. The signal flickered again, cutting in and out. "Yes, Dad, it's me!" she screamed into the phone. "I don't have much time, but you and Mom need to know I'm okay."

The static distorted part of his response, but she caught enough. "... told us you disappeared...Claire, what is going on? Where are you?"

"I can't explain right now," she answered quickly, her voice urgent. "But I'm fine...I'm safe."

A hard edge crept into her father's tone, his suspicion clear. "Why can't you tell me where you are? What happened?"

She wanted to tell him everything, to lay bare the whole horrible truth, but she knew she couldn't. Instead, she forced a lightness in her voice. "It's complicated, but I promise I'm being taken care of. I'm staying with a missionary. His name is Jack."

A second of silence. "A missionary?" The skepticism in his voice filled her with dread.

"Yes," she confirmed quickly. "He's here with me. I'm using his phone."

Another pause. "Put him on."

Claire handed the phone to Jack, her pulse pounding.

"Hello, Mr. Thompson," Jack said, his voice calm and

reassuring. "I'm Jack McKenzie. Claire has been staying at my orphanage. I promise you, I'm making sure she's looked after."

A few muffled words crackled through the connection, but Claire couldn't make them out. Frustrated, she snatched the phone back.

"Dad, listen to me. You *cannot* come to Kenya!" she pleaded. "It isn't safe."

A long crackling sound, then: "Why isn't it safe?"

She fought to steady her voice. "Just trust me, *please*! I'll explain everything when I get home in a few days."

"We need answers, Claire. We're not just going to sit back and—"

"Dad!" she cut in. "Whatever you do, don't come to—"

A sharp click. The line went dead.

Silence.

Claire froze, the phone still clutched in her hand. The emptiness of the moment crashed over her, and the only sound she heard was her own ragged breathing filling the void.

Jack placed a gentle hand on her shoulder. "It's going to be okay," he murmured. "He heard you. And even if he doesn't understand everything right now, I believe God will make it clear to him."

"I don't know, Jack," she whispered. "What if they still come? What if I couldn't stop them?"

He wrapped his arms around her, his hold firm. "You did everything you could," he reassured her. "And you're not alone in this."

She leaned into him, clutching the fabric of his shirt. The steady rhythm of his heartbeat calmed the spiraling thoughts in her head. They sat in silence on the rocky ledge, the vast beauty of the landscape stretching before them. For many minutes, they didn't speak.

Then Jack leaned in, his breath a warm caress against her cheek. "Claire," he murmured, "I wanted you to know…I've fallen in love with you."

She pulled back just enough to search his face—and in his

eyes, she found everything she needed.

A slow smile spread across her lips. "I love you, too, Jack."

His lips met hers in a kiss that was as soft as it was certain, wrapping them in a moment that belonged only to them.

As they pulled apart, Jack's fingers gently tucked her hair behind her ear. His gaze held hers, filled with quiet affection. "Ready to go?"

She nodded, letting the warmth of his presence steady her. With him by her side, her fears seemed to fade into the distance.

An hour later, Jack and Claire arrived at the Maasai village. She dismounted the motorcycle with a grateful sigh, wincing as pain shot through her arm. But even that couldn't dull her anticipation. Being here, being part of something bigger than herself, reminded her that this moment was all that mattered.

Jack rummaged through his backpack, pulling out a well-worn Kodak camera. "I know how much you love photography," he said, handing it to her. "Even with one hand, you should be able to operate it. I was hoping you could document the children and our work here."

She beamed, already imagining the stories she could tell through its lens.

"Thank you!" Then hesitating, she added, "But the Maasai don't allow pictures."

"You're right. They believe it can capture their souls," Jack explained. "But I've built trust with the chief. If I explain its purpose, I think he'll agree."

As they stepped into the village, Claire took in the sight before her—the warriors standing at the perimeter, spears in hand; the women adorned with colorful beads, their movements fluid and graceful. The scent of earth and distant cooking fires filled the air.

An elderly man stepped forward, his face deeply lined with wisdom. Jack greeted him in the melodic Maasai language, gesturing toward the camera. The chief studied it for a long moment before finally clasping Jack's hand in agreement.

Turning to Claire, Jack outlined her role. "Capture the

medical supplies, the children during treatments—anything that tells the story. But be respectful; if someone declines, move on."

She nodded. "Should I take before-and-after shots of the treatments?"

"Absolutely. And here," he pulled out a bag of candy "Hand these out for bravery."

As Claire moved carefully among the villagers, she was struck by what her lens captured—the quiet strength of a mother cradling her child, an elder resting a protective hand on a young warrior's shoulder, the unbreakable resilience in their faces.

But it was the children's red-rimmed, swollen eyes that affected her the most. As Jack administered the ointment, she was overwhelmed that something so small could save a child's sight.

By the time the last child was treated, Claire felt it deeply—a sense of purpose that went beyond medical care. This mission wasn't just about healing; it was about restoring dignity, offering hope, and showing compassion in a way that could change lives.

And she felt as if she was *meant* to be a part of it all.

She began to wonder if God had brought her here for this very moment, if everything she had been through had been shaping her for something greater.

As Claire and Jack rode back to the orphanage beneath the soft hues of sunset, a quiet peace settled over her. When she had first arrived in Kenya, she had been adrift in grief, unsure of where she belonged.

But now...she felt different. Brighter. Stronger.

The sorrow that had weighed her down for so long had been replaced by something new—purpose.

A comforting thought surfaced: *Tyler would be happy for me.*

He would have wanted her to embrace life fully, to cherish each moment with an open, unburdened heart.

She tightened her arms around Jack and whispered a silent prayer of thanks—for Jack, for this experience, and for the winding path that had led her here.

Chapter 31

Intruder at the Orphanage

When Claire and Jack arrived back at the orphanage, Sadie greeted them at the door, her steps lighter than before. She led them to the dining room, where a modest meal was set out.

The tear stains that had once marked her cheeks were gone, replaced by a quiet brightness in her eyes—a gentle glow that spoke of hope finding its way back in.

As they settled down, Sadie took a breath. "I bought a plane ticket home. I'm leaving next week for Georgia."

Jack opened his mouth to respond, but she lifted a hand, stopping him. "No, Jack. You won't talk me out of it. I've made up my mind. I know I'm breakin' my commitment here, but every minute with Mark is a gift, and I'm not gonna let him go through this alone."

Silence stretched between them. Sadie braced herself, as if expecting an argument.

But then Jack smiled. "Sadie, you don't need to apologize. *I'm* the one who's sorry. I should never have pressured you to stay. It was selfish. You should be with Mark, and I'm glad you're going home."

He glanced at Claire, his voice softer. "It's important to cherish every moment with the people you love."

Tears welled in Sadie's eyes as she stood abruptly and pulled him into a fierce hug. Claire felt a sense of relief at the sight of them—two friends, understanding each other without bitterness.

The evening passed in a blur of laughter and warm conversation, but as the night wound down, Jack's tone grew serious.

"Tomorrow afternoon, Claire and I will leave for Nairobi," he announced. Silence fell over the table. "I've already arranged for friends to come by and help while I'm gone."

No one responded right away. Instead, they remained at the table, a heavy silence stretching between them. When goodnights were finally exchanged, their hugs held on just a little longer—reluctant to let go.

As Claire slipped beneath her blanket, its familiar weight offered little comfort. She had spent so much time preparing for this moment, convincing herself she was ready to return home. But now that it was here, saying goodbye felt overwhelming, like a tide pulling her under.

Sleep didn't come easily. Every time she closed her eyes, a dull ache settled in her chest, reminding her of everything she was about to leave behind.

Then, a voice, muffled and tight, drifted in from somewhere outside her room. Something in its strained tone set her on edge. Her heart pounded as she tried to tell herself it was nothing. But she couldn't shake the unease.

She threw off the covers, slid out of bed, and stepped into the darkened hallway.

Claire found Jack pacing in the living room, his hands tight on his hips, his movements sharp and agitated. Patrick, the old Maasai guard, stood nearby, his usually steady eyes clouded with worry.

"You did the right thing getting me," Jack said, his voice low and clipped. "I didn't call for a doctor."

Patrick was about to reply when he spotted her. "Miss, why are you out of bed?"

Jack's head snapped toward her, surprise flashing across his face. "Claire, you need to return to your room until we know what's going on."

She crossed her arms, her chin set. "I don't think so. We both know this has something to do with me. I'm not going to hide and wait to see what happens."

For a flash, he looked like he was battling a storm of words. Then, a wry amusement softened his eyes. "Of course not," he sighed.

Turning to Patrick, he asked, "What happened after you told him to wait outside the gate while you checked?"

"As soon as I turned around to go get you," he reported. "I heard his motorcycle start up, and he rode off. I'm not sure where he went."

"Can you describe him?" Jack asked.

"He was white, younger than me, with bright red hair. Dressed in all black. His eyes…they were cold and mean-looking."

Claire gasped loudly. The man from Narok!

Jack was at her side in an instant. "Claire, what is it? Are you okay?"

She swallowed against the rising panic. "I've seen that man before. In Narok. He was following me…watching me."

"It looks like he's been tracking you," Jack uttered, his expression grim.

Her stomach twisted. *Tracking me…?*

Jack straightened, his whole body shifting into high alert. "We need to act fast."

Without another word, he strode from the room, disappearing down the hallway. Seconds later, he returned, leading Sadie into the dimly lit space. She yawned, rubbing at her eyes as Jack quickly briefed her on the situation.

"So, what do you think is the best course of action?" Jack asked the group. "Do we check the fence, see if there's any sign that he's gotten inside? Or lock ourselves in with the children?"

"I will check the gate and fence," Patrick responded firmly. "It's my job to make sure this orphanage stays safe. If there's no damage or sign that he entered, then we'll know he's gone."

Jack gave a quick nod. "I agree. But you'll need help. Alright, Sadie and Claire—you two stay here with the children while Patrick and I check the fence and—"

"I'm coming with you," Claire interrupted, her voice like steel.

"Claire, this man is most likely after you," Jack said, his voice urgent. "It's too dangerous for you to be outside while he's out there somewhere."

"Then I definitely can't stay here," she countered. "If he gets inside, the kids will be at risk."

A beat of tense silence followed.

Then Sadie, still blinking away sleep, stepped forward. "Claire's right, Jack," she murmured. "If this man is after her, she should stay with you. The children would be safer that way. I'll gather them into the back room until you return."

Jack's jaw clenched tightly, but then with a reluctant sigh, he said, "Okay."

Turning to Patrick, he instructed, "Patrick, check the gate and east side, and Claire and I will cover the west."

Claire wasted no time. She turned and practically flew back to her room. Her hands shook as she dressed, but she didn't slow down. She grabbed a flashlight from the kitchen and hurried back to the living room. Jack was already there, waiting.

Their eyes locked.

No words were needed—only the quiet certainty that whatever lay ahead, they would face it together.

As they stepped outside, the night wrapped around them like a thick blanket of eerie silence, broken only by the distant cry of an unknown animal. The flashlight beam pierced the darkness, illuminating the path ahead, but it did little to push back Claire's nerves.

Beside her, Jack moved with determination, alert, ready for danger. They crept along the fence inspecting it for any signs of tampering. Then the flashlight caught something.

A motorcycle.

It was propped against the base of a tree where a low—

hanging branch bent toward the ground.

Jack's fingers curled around her wrist, his grip instinctive, protective. But before either of them could move, the night erupted in a deafening roar.

A gunshot!

The sound split the air like a jagged crack of thunder, rattling Claire to her core. Her lungs seized. The flashlight slipped from her grip, hitting the dirt with a muffled thud, plunging them into complete darkness.

"Was that a g-gunshot?" she whispered.

"Yes!" Jack answered as he snatched the flashlight from the ground. "The children!"

Jack's fingers locked around hers, pulling her forward. They sprinted back toward the orphanage, a sharp rush of adrenaline coursing through them, the crack of gunfire still ringing in their ears.

The moment they reached the building, they rushed to the back room where the children were hiding. Jack threw open the door, his gaze sweeping the darkness.

Claire's eyes adjusted just in time to see it. A dark shape, sleek and silent, sliding along the far wall.

Then a raw, animalistic cry tore through the room, shattering the quiet.

Before Claire could even draw breath to scream, a sudden whoosh cut through the air, swift and deadly.

Chapter 32

Patrick's Bravery

The figure surged forward, a blur of motion. "You will not lay a finger on these children!"

"It's me, Sadie! It's me!" Jack shouted, throwing up his arms in defense.

The club slipped from Sadie's hands and hit the floor with a thud. Her knees buckled, and she crumpled, all the fight draining out of her in an instant.

Claire dropped to her side, gripping Sadie's hands—small, clammy, ice-cold. "It's okay. You're safe," she whispered, though her own pulse was still racing.

Jack's hand settled on Claire's shoulder. "I think you should stay here. I'll go and find Patrick."

Claire was about to protest, but then she looked into Sadie's terrified eyes, and the children huddled in the corner, and she knew she couldn't leave them.

"Yes. Go!" she urged him. "We'll be fine here."

Jack slipped out of the door and vanished into the night.

Time slowed to a crawl, each second a torture. Every sound—the floor creaking, fabric rustling—sent Claire's heart leaping into her throat.

She cradled a sleeping toddler in her lap, her fingers moving nervously through the soft curls. But the child's warmth couldn't chase away the cold dread that gripped her.

She waited, and she prayed—that Jack would return.

At last, the door swung open. Jack stepped in, his silhouette stark against the dim light, his face lined with exhaustion.

The grip of fear that had held Claire captive melted away, replaced by a wave of relief.

"It's alright," Jack announced, his voice weary. "The danger has passed. Go on back to your beds now. Older children, please help the younger ones."

The children obeyed, though their steps were slow, eyes darting to the darkened windows as if someone might leap through.

Jack turned to Claire and Sadie. "Come with me."

They followed him into the living room, where the oil lamp cast flickering silhouettes across the worn furniture, adding an unsettling air to the already tense atmosphere.

They sank onto a lumpy couch. Jack's voice was hard with a nervous edge, as he began to recount what had happened.

"I was searching for Patrick at the gate when I heard moaning. I ran toward the sound and there he was. On the ground, blood running down his temple. A bullet had grazed his temple."

Sadie let out a loud gasp, and Claire pressed a shaky hand to her mouth.

Jack raised a hand, his expression calm but firm. "It wasn't deep," he reassured them. "He said he found the intruder while walking the fence. The man pointed a gun at him, demanding to know if Claire was here."

Claire's blood ran cold as she absorbed his words. "I knew this was about me."

Jack nodded grimly. "Yes. He was after you. But Patrick is a Maasai warrior," he continued, something like admiration in his voice. "He reacted with instinct sharpened by years of protecting his tribe. He grabbed his club from his belt and threw it at the man's head. It hit its mark, causing the gun to go off. Both of them hit the ground, and by the time Patrick came to, the intruder was gone."

Claire shuddered, a sick feeling curdling in her stomach.

"When I found him," Jack continued, "he was just sitting on the ground, disoriented. I took him home to his wife. Tomorrow, she'll take him to the clinic, but I think he's going to be okay."

"God saved him…and us," Sadie murmured.

"Yes," Jack agreed. "This was God's protection." Then, his eyes shifted to Claire. "It's not safe for you here anymore. We're not going to wait until tomorrow afternoon. As soon as the sun comes up, we're leaving for Nairobi."

She barely heard him. Her mind was trapped in the image of Patrick—crumpled on the ground, blood trickling down his face.

Because of me.

Jack placed a reassuring hand on her shoulder. "Claire, it's natural to feel shaken by what's happened, but try to get some rest."

"But it was *my* fault that Patrick was hurt."

"This is *not* your fault," Jack assured her. "Patrick chose to protect the orphanage. To protect all of us."

Tears welled up in her eyes as she nodded.

"Okay. Let's get to bed," Jack said as he stood. "We have a long day tomorrow."

Claire faltered for a moment, then whispered, "Jack, I'd feel safer if you stayed with me…just for a while. That man…is still out there somewhere."

His expression softened. "Of course. As long as you need."

He led her to her room. The candle's glow bathed the space in warmth, but it couldn't chase away the terror of the night.

She sat on the edge of the bed, her body heavy with exhaustion. Jack settled beside her, wrapping an arm around her shoulder.

"Come here," he murmured, drawing her close.

She leaned into him, letting the steady beat of his heartbeat anchor her, the warmth of his body offering a comfort she so desperately needed.

"Thank you for staying," she whispered. "I don't know what I'd do without you."

Jack was silent for a long time. When he finally spoke, his voice held a deep pain that caught her off guard.

"I know you have to leave tomorrow, Claire. It's just…I can't imagine this place without you."

The raw ache in his voice unraveled something deep inside her, loosening threads she hadn't realized were wound so tight. She tried to speak, but the words caught, trapped in her throat.

So, they sat side by side on the bed, the silence heavy with everything they couldn't bring themselves to say.

Then, the candle sputtered…then again…before surrendering to the darkness.

Their final hours together slipped away—fragile, fleeting, like wisps of smoke carried on the wind.

Chapter 33

A Risky Gamble

Bang!

The gunshot shattered the silence, ripping through the night.

Claire bolted upright, her breath coming in ragged gasps, her heart hammering against her ribs. Disoriented, she clutched the blanket, her eyes darting around.

For a moment, she struggled to separate her dream from reality. But as the tightness in her chest eased, truth settled in—she was safe. The danger had passed.

Somewhere outside, a rooster crowed, the ordinary sound pulling her further from the nightmare's grip.

She exhaled slowly and reached beside her, seeking comfort in Jack's presence. Her fingers met only cool, empty space.

He was gone.

The warmth of his body had long since faded, but the blanket tucked snugly around her whispered of his care.

Sitting upright, a flood of memories rushed back—the fear, the gunshot, the agonizing wait for Jack to return. Yet beneath it all, a quiet certainty held firm: they had been protected.

She dressed quickly, then slipped into the hallway, her purpose clear—she needed to find Jack.

The scent of freshly baked bread and brewing coffee

enveloped her as she stepped into the kitchen. The warmth of the morning routine felt almost soothing—until a tap on her shoulder startled her, causing her to whirl around.

Jack stood there, fatigue etched into his face. His tousled blond hair, the faint smudge of dirt on his cheek, and the slight slump of his shoulders hinted at an early morning of hard work. He looked exhausted, but still, somehow, he managed a small smile.

"Good morning," he murmured.

Claire's heart softened. "You look like you've been up for hours."

He exhaled, rubbing the back of his neck. "Never went to bed, actually. Had a few things to handle before we left for Nairobi. I hope you don't mind."

She shook her head, reaching up instinctively to smooth a stray strand of his hair back into place. "Why would I mind?"

He leaned in, his voice low, meant only for her. "I hated leaving you this morning," he admitted, his fingers brushing lightly against hers. "There's nothing I want more than to hold you in my arms."

A quiet thrill raced through her at the tenderness in his voice. Instead of answering, she gently squeezed his hand, letting the warmth of her touch say what words couldn't.

Soon, breakfast was served, the cheerful chatter of the orphans filling the space. Claire felt lighter as she watched them giggle and nudge each other, a quiet but powerful reminder of the resilience of young hearts.

Sadie dropped into the seat beside her with a long dramatic sigh. The dark circles under her eyes betrayed her exhaustion, and she barely touched her food, offering only weak smiles and half-hearted words.

Then groaning loudly, she said, "I have to say, ya'll, I'm a bundle of nerves!" Her Southern twang seemed to reach new heights. "I don't think I can take something like that again! And I didn't sleep a wink either. I just laid there, plumb worn out, waiting for something else bad to happen!"

Claire reached over, giving Sadie's hand a gentle squeeze. "I get it, Sadie. Last night was terrifying. But it's over now. We're safe." She hesitated, her voice softening. "And once I'm gone, things should calm down around here. You won't have to worry anymore."

With a long sigh, Sadie leaned back in her chair. "Thanks, Claire, I know all that in my head. It's just that my nerves haven't gotten the memo!"

Jack chuckled, a low, soothing rumble. Claire's own laugh slipped out, surprising her—it felt almost foreign, like a forgotten melody finding its way back to her.

Sadie's expression fell. "And I hate that you're leaving today, Claire. I'll miss you so much."

Claire pulled her into a hug. "We'll find a way to stay in touch. I promise."

Sadie's arms tightened around her. "You'd better. After Mark's treatments, I expect a visit. You hear?"

Claire managed a small laugh. "You've got it."

After breakfast, Jack left to pick up his friends, promising to return quickly.

Claire busied herself with preparations. She brushed her hair and tied it back into a sleek ponytail, each pull of the band a quiet attempt to hold herself together.

Sadie had generously gifted her a simple skirt and blouse, along with a pair of sandals—sparing her the need to wear the tattered dress the Maasai woman had given her.

Sitting on the edge of her bed, Claire smoothed the fabric of the borrowed skirt. As her fingers absently traced the stitching, her heart filled with gratitude.

The Maasai warriors who saved her. The woman who nursed her back to health. Sadie and the children. Jack. Each of them had been instrumental—not just in her survival, but in her healing.

But as the morning light filtered through the window, a shadow fell over her thoughts. The warmth of thankfulness began to cool, edged out by the uncertainty surrounding her upcoming statement to the police.

She desperately wanted those men caught, and held accountable. But without concrete evidence, would her story be dismissed as paranoia—or worse, mere imagination?

She thought of the flash drive, tucked away in the girls' dormitory—the evidence she'd risked her life to protect. That photo revealed the poachers' secretive dealings, their faces, and even the merchandise. Without it, would the police even take her seriously?

She was still lost in thought when she heard the front door open. Jack's voice mingled with the deeper ones of his friends, who had come to help in his absence.

Claire stepped into the front room and motioned for him to follow her. Once inside her room, she closed the door.

"Jack," she said, her voice barely above a whisper, "we need to talk about something before we go to the police station."

"Is everything alright?" he asked, detecting the strain in her voice. "Did something happen while I was away?"

"No, I'm fine," she reassured him, although her nerves twisting in her stomach told a different story. "I've been thinking...I think we should stop by my campus to get my flash drive before going to the police."

His forehead creased. "Claire, it's not safe there—"

"I know," she cut in, rushing to explain. "But I'm not sure the police will take me seriously without proof. It has what I need to convince them of what I saw."

Jack shifted uneasily, his apprehension clear. "But why can't you just tell the officers where you hid it? Why put yourself in danger to get it yourself?"

"I thought about that," she responded. "But I hid it so well. Honestly, I'm not sure they'd even bother searching for it, let alone find it. But I know *exactly* where it is."

She paused, choosing her words carefully. "Jack, those men believed that photo was so damning that they destroyed my phone and laptop because of it. They knew it could take them down. Don't you think it's worth the risk in order to stop them for good?"

He looked away, his hands pressing against his hips as he stared at the floor. "I don't know, Claire." He shook his head. "I've been telling you for days that the campus isn't safe. And now, after nearly losing you last night, I'm supposed to just take you back there?"

She steadied her breathing, forcing herself to stay composed. "I know it's a gamble. But if we don't try, those men could get away with everything they've done. We might be the only ones who can stop them."

Her voice dropped, tight with desperation. "And you know they won't stop hurting innocent animals and people until somebody puts an end to it."

Jack's whole body seemed to tense under the weight of the decision. "I hate this plan...but I also hate the idea of those men walking free."

Claire stepped closer, her palm resting gently against his chest. "I wouldn't ask if I didn't believe we could pull this off without too much risk," she said, her eyes locked onto his. "If we go around one when everyone's at lunch, the campus would be empty. I can slip into my room and grab it—five minutes, tops. No one will even know we were there."

He let out a long, measured breath. "Alright. I'll trust you on this. But if anything feels off," he added, a steely edge to his voice. "We're gone. No hesitation."

Jack's hand moved to cradle her face, his touch gentle, almost as if afraid she might break. His voice dropped to a whisper. "I can't lose you, Claire."

Her response was wordless. She leaned in, pressing her lips to his—a silent promise, a quiet thank you.

A moment later, they pulled apart, the warmth of the moment filling them both with the courage they needed to face what lay ahead.

Back in the living room, Jack gave instructions to his friends while Claire exchanged a tearful goodbye with Sadie.

Then she embraced each orphan, their small bodies

clinging to hers as if seeking comfort. "I'll try to return one day," she murmured faintly.

As they rode away on Jack's motorcycle, Claire cast one last glance at the House of Hope. She wanted to freeze the scene— to hold onto the safety, the kindness, the sense of belonging she had found there.

But as the orphanage disappeared behind them, swallowed by the vast Kenyan landscape, a sudden unease stirred within her. She had been so sure this plan was worth the risk, but now, doubt started to creep in.

Did I make a mistake convincing Jack to do this? she fretted. *What if we're walking straight into danger?*

The road ahead stretched out before her, cloaked in uncertainty, much like the unsettling thoughts racing through her mind.

Chapter 34

Covert Mission

As Jack and Claire neared her campus, the midday sun beat down on them, a deep contrast to the cold knot of dread lodged in Claire's chest.

Jack guided his motorcycle behind a dense thicket of shrubs, cutting the engine. They hopped off and crouched near the fence. Usually bustling with students, the campus now sat eerily quiet during the lunch break.

Jack kept his voice low. "We need a plan. We can't just stroll up to the gate like a couple of tourists. How do we get past the guard?"

Claire hesitated for a moment. She had been so certain before—but now, with the campus right in front of her, the risks pressed in from all sides.

What if this is all a mistake?

Jack's voice pulled her from her thoughts. "Claire?"

She let out a slow breath. There was no turning back now. "The guard might recognize me," she murmured. "But you're a stranger. You could ask for something. Maybe a donation for the orphanage. If he believes you and opens the gate, you'll need to distract him long enough for me to slip past."

"How should I do that?"

"Something subtle," she suggested. "Knock over a sign or drop something near his feet—just enough to make him turn away. If he's focused on you, I can sneak past."

He nodded but worry clouded his expression. "Okay. I'll give it my best shot. But if he catches on, things could go south fast."

She squeezed his hand. "We've come too far to back out now." Her voice was steadier than she felt. "You've got this."

Jack swung onto his motorcycle, and with a quick twist of the throttle, he roared down the road and around the bend, leaving Claire alone.

Her pulse pounded as she crept along the fence, positioning herself near the gate. Every nerve in her body was a live wire, ready to spring the moment she saw an opening.

Moments later, Jack emerged from the shadows, his stride casual as he approached the guard at the entrance. Claire held her breath, watching as he spoke, producing something from his wallet—credentials, maybe?

The guard's expression shifted, hesitancy in his face. Then, to her relief, the guard opened the gate and Jack stepped through.

This is it!

She darted forward, hugging the fence line. Just as she neared the entrance, the guard's hand started to move toward the gate. A second more and her chance would be gone.

Then Jack let out a strangled cry and collapsed. He clutched his ankle, his face contorted in apparent agony. His anguished cries echoed across the quiet campus, snapping the guard's attention to him.

Claire slipped through the gate like a phantom, then sprinted towards the girls' dormitory. Each step felt like an eternity, adrenaline driving her forward.

When she finally reached the safety of the building, she hugged the wall, staying in the shadows. She cast a glance over her shoulder. Jack was still on the ground, writhing in pain, the guard crouched beside him, his back turned.

A few minutes later, Jack appeared by her side, his face flushed, breathing hard.

"He's gone…to get help," he whispered, his voice ragged

but triumphant.

"Subtle," she murmured with a small smile.

Jack smirked. "What can I say? I commit to the role."

But as he checked his watch, his expression sobered. "We've got ten minutes until lunch is over."

"That's enough," she whispered. "I'll go in and grab the flash drive while you keep guard here. Then we'll sneak out the same way we came in."

All of a sudden, Jack's phone vibrated, its low, insistent buzz slicing through the silence like a blade.

Claire's eyes widened in alarm. "Turn it off!" she hissed.

He fumbled for the phone, but his fingers froze when he saw the caller ID. "It's your dad," he whispered.

"What?" Her voice was barely audible, shock written all over her face.

Jack hesitated, only for a second, then answered. "Hello, Mr. Thompson," he whispered. "I can't talk right now."

A strained voice crackled through the speaker. "Is Claire with you? Is she okay?"

Her father's tone was rigid, urgent—something didn't sound right.

"Yes, she's fine," he responded, keeping his voice low.

"We just stepped—" her father began.

Before he could finish, Jack cut him off with a swift tap, ending the call.

Claire was about to protest, but his expression stopped her. He wasn't looking at her anymore; his gaze was locked on the entrance.

The guard had returned.

The man's keen eyes swept the area, his posture stiff with suspicion.

Seconds stretched agonizingly as the guard scanned the campus. Then with a loud, definitive clang, he locked the gate back into place.

Jack and Claire pressed themselves flat against the wall, barely daring to breathe. Every beat of Claire's heart echoed the fear that the guard might see them.

Then Jack glanced at his watch and slowly held up seven fingers.

Seven minutes left.

The clock was ticking.

She had no time to waste. If they were going to succeed, she had to move—now.

Steeling herself, she crept forward. Then in one fluid motion, she slipped through the doorway, vanishing inside like a wisp of smoke.

She quickly scanned the dormitory. Empty.

Finding her tweezers, she hurried to the narrow crack in the wall. Desperation sharpened her movements, guiding her hand with surprising precision as she carefully pried the flash drive free and slipped it into her pocket.

As she turned to leave, a glint of something under her bed caught her eye. It was her camera, its familiar shape lay partially hidden in the shadows.

She hesitated, but only for a second.

No. I can't leave it.

She dropped to her knees, stretching her hand under the bed. Just as her fingers closed around the camera's familiar contours—

A voice shattered the silence.

"Claire."

Her name, spoken gently but with unmistakable emotion, sent a shock through her.

She shot to her feet and whirled around.

Peter Miller stood in the doorway, a wide smile lighting his face.

"I can't believe it's you!" he exclaimed, closing the distance between them. "I've been searching everywhere for you."

Without a second thought, she rushed forward, throwing her arms around him in a tight embrace, the urgency of her mission momentarily overshadowed by the relief of seeing a familiar face.

He held her closely, his voice dipping to a whisper near her ear. "What happened to you? Where have you been all this time?"

His questions snapped her back to reality. "It's a long story, Peter," she said as she pulled away. "But I could really use your help."

"Of course," he replied, his voice light and casual. "What do you want me to do?"

"I need to find another way off campus," she said quickly, her words tumbling out. "I can't use the front entrance."

Her fingers brushed the cool metal of the flash drive in her pocket, a tangible reminder of why she was there. She was about to show him—

But then she stopped.

Something felt wrong.

Peter was a friend—an ally. Someone she could trust. Right?

And yet...

A sudden cold enveloped her, causing her breath to catch in her throat.

How did Peter know I was here?

Chapter 35

The Mastermind

With a barely perceptible movement, Claire released the flash drive and slowly withdrew her hand from her pocket.

Peter's sudden presence triggered an alarm within her, like a whisper of danger brushing against her thoughts.

"Peter," she stated cautiously, forcing her voice to remain steady. "How did you know I'd be here?"

He smiled, like he was amused by the question. "It wasn't hard." His tone suggested the answer was obvious. "The guards and I are all friends. When Jed came to tell me a missionary was at the gate, I figured you'd come with him."

The casual mention of Jack sent a quick, electric tingle up the back of her neck. "But how could you know I'd be with a missionary?" she pressed.

Peter sighed, as if growing tired of the game. The amiable mask he had been wearing cracked, his features twisting with irritation.

"Claire, don't act so surprised. I found your little hiding spot days ago. An orphanage? Really?"

His voice took on a hard edge. "When my colleague failed to find you last night, I made sure the guards were on alert. I told them to notify me if a missionary showed up," his lips curled into a cruel smirk, "because I knew you wouldn't be far behind.

His words hit her like a hammer blow. The room swayed,

and her knees wobbled. She stared at him, grappling to reconcile the person before her with the man she thought she knew.

The professor she leaned on for guidance. The friend who shared her love of photography. The person she trusted with her secret.

The betrayal she never saw coming.

"Was it...you?" The words constricted her throat. "Were you the one outside the hut? The one who ordered those men to..."

She couldn't finish.

Peter's expression remained unchanged. No denial. No regret.

The cruelty etched in his face was all the confirmation she needed. He was the mastermind—the one pulling the strings behind the entire poaching ring.

Across from her, his smile widened, cold and predatory. "Let's just say I don't like loose ends."

Then, twisting the knife deeper, he added, "And in case you're wondering, my redheaded friend was hurt quite badly with that club. He's in the hospital recovering." A glint of something dangerous danced in his eyes. "I don't like it when my friends get hurt."

Peter wasn't just capable of violence, he thrived on it.

Her gaze darted to the door, hoping she could somehow get away—make a break for it.

But before she could move, Peter's eyes narrowed, and in an instant, he stepped into her path, cutting off any chance of escape.

Cornered and desperate, another thought struck her. "Where's Jack?" she shrieked.

The sneer on Peter's face intensified. "Your new boyfriend? Don't worry; he's in good hands."

Turning to the door, he called out, "Johnny!"

A man stepped into the dormitory—the same man from the hut, the one from the photo.

"Where's the missionary?" he demanded.

"Knocked him out cold, Boss," Johnny announced, a twisted grin spreading across his face. "Carl is hauling him to the shed. He's gonna have one wicked headache when he wakes up... *if* he wakes up."

He laughed, the sound sharp and grating. "I might've gotten a little carried away, but hey, you never complain about a little extra convincing, right?"

Her breath came in short, shallow bursts.

No. No, no, no.

She lunged forward. She *had* to find Jack!

But Peter's iron grip yanked her back causing her camera to slip from her hands, falling to the floor with a final, heartbreaking crash.

Peter's gaze shifted to the broken device. "Ah, your *precious* camera. I thought I might've tipped my hand when I told you I love to shoot animals! It was a little joke, you see. I *do* love to shoot animals...just not with a camera."

A humorless laugh echoed through the room. Peter leaned in, his voice curling into a sinister whisper. "And that incident at the lodge...when I ran into one of my customers? Let's just say he wasn't too happy with the new terms of our agreement." His tone shifted, almost gloating, as if this were all just a game. "But after a little, um, persuasion, he understood the consequences of disloyalty."

Claire remembered the way the man's face at the lodge had turned white when Peter whispered something in his ear—the way he fled, fear carved into every line of his expression.

She thought of how easily Peter had sown doubt, making her question whether she'd really heard anything about a tusk exchange. How he'd urged her to keep quiet, persuading her not to tell anyone what she'd heard or seen.

And the way he'd looked her straight in the eye, promising the poachers would never come for a student—that she would be safe.

How could I have been so blind? So utterly fooled?

The truth snapped into focus. Every lie, each careful

manipulation, had been woven together into the perfect trap.

His smirk widened, as if he could read the horror etched on her face. "You see, pretty girls are my weakness," he gloated. "Each semester, I pick a new one, and you were going to be my next conquest. I even tried to convince you to stay with me that night. I had other ideas, of course."

His voice dropped to a menacing growl. "But you didn't stay, did you? You had to get all nosy. I still can't fathom what possessed you to take a picture of that meeting. Doesn't matter. You're caught in my web now."

His fingers dug into her chin, jerking her face toward his. The cruelty in his blue eyes sent a chill through her, freezing the blood in her veins.

"Now," he hissed, "you *are* going to tell me why you came back here."

Even as her pulse thundered like a drumbeat, she pressed her lips together, refusing to speak. She would *never* reveal the flash drive's location, *never* give him that satisfaction.

Peter's face darkened. "You don't want to talk? That's fine. I've got a little surprise for you, and once you hear it, I'm sure you'll tell me everything I want to know."

He turned to Johnny. "Get her to the shed before the campus is swarmed with students. We'll continue our little chat there."

As Peter pushed her forward, a gleam of metal caught her eye. In Johnny's hand was the unmistakable silhouette of a gun, and its barrel was aimed right at her.

"Let's go," Johnny sneered.

Claire followed him out of the dorm. With each step across the deserted campus, she felt the cold steel against her back, a constant reminder of how close death lurked.

As they neared the shed, she thought she saw a slight movement at the edge of her vision. But the shadow disappeared as quickly as it had appeared, leaving her uncertain if it was real or just a trick of her mind.

Johnny unlocked the shed door and flung it open. Without

warning, he shoved her forward. She stumbled, landing hard on the rough floor.

The door banged shut behind her, the ominous sound rippling through the silence.

Claire lay motionless, the cold, gritty surface pressing against her cheek as the harsh reality of her situation sank in.

But beneath the terror, a flicker of defiance sputtered to life.

Jack was here.
Injured.
Alone.
And he needed her.

Chapter 36

Friend or Foe

"Jack!" Her voice, raw with desperation, tore through the eerie silence of the shed. "Jack, where are you?"

Forcing her body into motion, she dragged herself forward, every movement slow and excruciating with one arm trapped in a sling. The rough, unforgiving floor scraped against her skin as she reached out, her fingers searching—hoping.

She strained to hear anything—a wheeze, a groan, the faintest sign of life. But the darkness absorbed every sound, turning the search into a blind, agonizing crawl through an unfamiliar maze.

At last, her hand brushed against something solid.

A body.

Leaning closer, she pressed her ear to the figure's chest, listening for any sign of life. She held her breath—until she finally heard it.

Thump—thump. Thump—thump.

He was alive!

Her hands flew to his face, tracing its contours, her fingers skimming over the familiar line of his jaw, his cheekbones, the rough stubble that dusted his chin.

Jack.

He was battered. Unconscious.

But alive.

"Thank you, God!" she whispered, as she cradled Jack's

head in her lap. Relief flooded through her, but it was fleeting, gone as quickly as it came.

Her fingers landed on something sticky and warm. The sharp, metallic tang of blood filled her senses.

A choked sob escaped her as the realization hit—her hands were covered in Jack's blood.

She cupped his face, her touch gentle but urgent. "Jack," she whispered. "Stay with me."

Claire leaned down and pressed a kiss to his forehead, and as she did, a faint moan gurgled from his throat.

"I'm here," she whispered, her voice breaking. "I've got you."

In that moment, she did the only thing she could. She prayed.

"God, please help us," she whispered into the darkness. "We need a miracle."

A flood of memories surged through her, dragging her back into the shadows of everything she'd survived.

Powerless in the suffocating confines of the kidnapper's hideout.

Bound and abandoned to die in the savanna.

The frantic flight from the snapping jaws of the hyenas.

Clinging to the tree through the endless, terror-filled night.

Desperately trying to convince the Maasai warriors to seek help.

The intruder stalking her at the orphanage.

In all those moments, she had felt helpless—trapped, with no way out.

But God had been there. Every time.

Comforting her. Guiding her. Protecting her.

A warmth blossomed inside her, pushing back against the cold dread that gripped her.

He saved me then. He WILL save us now.

In the stillness, a peace wrapped around her—a promise that they were not alone, that they had not been abandoned.

Suddenly, a burst of light pierced the gloom, flooding the shed as the door swung open. Claire flinched, her tear-filled eyes blinking rapidly against the harsh glare.

Someone parted the heavy curtain in front of the grimy window, sending dust swirling through the stagnant air. As her vision adjusted, three figures emerged from the light—Peter, Johnny, and a third man, presumably Carl.

Claire drew in a sharp breath. Carl was the man who had left her to die in the savanna.

The door slammed shut behind them, the sound reverberating like a death knell.

Peter stalked forward, his face twisted with something dark, something cruel. He crouched in front of her, too close, his presence suffocating. The smug smile curling his lips was as cold and dangerous as the man himself.

"Why did you come back here?" His voice was low, almost a whisper. "You *are* going to tell me."

Claire intensified her grip on Jack, her silence an act of rebellion.

Peter's smirk vanished. His eyes narrowed into thin slits. When he spoke again, his voice was razor-sharp.

"Here's my surprise." He paused for a few seconds, letting the silence coil around her like a noose. "Your parents are here in Kenya."

Her stomach bottomed out, a sickening free fall that left her dizzy.

Oh God...No!

"My parents...are here?" Her words felt brittle in the heavy air. But even as she said it, the truth was evident.

Of course, they would come. Nothing could have kept them away. They would need to see her, touch her—make sure that she was safe.

Her lungs seized, the air turning to stone in her chest.

Peter continued, his tone mockingly calm. "The Dean informed the staff they'd be arriving around dinnertime."

He leaned in, savoring the moment, and delivered the final

blow. "And when they get here," he snarled, "I'm going to make sure they regret the day they ever set foot on this campus."

He let the threat settle, allowing it to seep in before adding, "Unless, of course, you tell me what I want to know."

The ultimatum struck like a wrecking ball, shattering through everything she loved. Her parents were now in danger, walking straight into a trap—all because of their love.

And now, she was faced with an impossible choice.

Tell Peter about the flash drive and gamble that the truth would be enough to save her parents. Or lie, and possibly doom them all.

Her throat constricted, each breath a painful squeeze. She knew what she had to do.

"I...I came back for my camera."

His expression contorted with disbelief. "Your camera?" he spat. "Are you seriously telling me you risked everything to come back for that asinine camera? Do you think I'm an idiot?"

"But I did!" she shot back. "You know I love photography. That camera means everything to me!"

Peter stared at her, silent. Calculating.

Then he straightened. His voice curt. "Stand up. Turn out your pockets."

A cold rush of terror seized her. The flash drive in her pocket felt like a ticking time bomb.

She rose slowly, forcing her shaking hand into her pocket. Her fingers closed tightly around the device. With deliberate care, she pulled the pocket inside out, the drive hidden in her closed palm.

His unyielding gaze bore into hers. She willed her body to stay still, even as her heart pounded like a drum against her ribs.

"Turn out the other pocket," he demanded.

"My other arm is broken," she said coldly, "thanks to you. So you'll have to check it yourself."

With a dismissive grunt, he reached into her pocket, rummaging briefly before withdrawing empty-handed.

Satisfied, he turned to Johnny. "Go to the dorm and get

her camera. It's already broken, but I want to make sure it never works again."

A scream tore through her throat. "But why!"

His cruel grin widened. "Because you wanted it."

Then, with chilling finality, he barked, "Carl, get the truck. It's time we say goodbye to Miss Thompson and her... unfortunate companion."

A strangled groan erupted from Jack, his weakened voice pulling Claire's attention back to him. She jolted when she saw him—curled in a fetal position on the ground, his blood matted into his hair and trickling slowly down his cheek.

Peter's voice was cold and taunting. "Enjoy your last minutes together."

With a vicious shove, he sent her stumbling toward Jack. Her knees hit the ground, pain shooting up her legs.

She scrambled over to Jack, wrapping her arms around him, as if her embrace alone could shield him from the horrors that awaited them.

Then she caught a glimpse of movement outside the grimy window.

Her breath suddenly hitched, as Daniel's face emerged from the shadows. He stood at the window, his face half-hidden, when his eyes locked onto hers. There was something in his look—something she couldn't decipher.

For a single electrifying moment, time seemed to freeze. Her heart lurched, hope and terror colliding in her chest.

Is he here to save me or betray me?

But before she could unravel his intentions, he vanished as quickly as he had appeared.

In an instant, the hope of rescue, of a miracle, vanished. Despair crowded her thoughts, whispering that all was lost.

Yet beneath the fear, a truth like a steady flame emerged. Even now, even here, God had not abandoned her.

If rescue didn't come, then courage would.

If the darkness closed in, then His light would meet her there.

And in the silence, she whispered a prayer. Not for escape…but for strength.

Suddenly, a deafening crack tore through the air as the shed door slammed open. Both Peter and Claire's heads snapped toward the sound.

Daniel stood in the doorway, rage twisting his face into something unrecognizable.

The metallic glint of Johnny's gun, held steady in his hand, gleamed with deadly intent.

Chapter 37

Battle in the Shed

Daniel's eyes burned with a terrifying intensity as he swept the room, every muscle taut and ready.

With a snarl, Peter launched himself at Daniel, closing the distance between them before Daniel could even aim the weapon. It was a reckless, dangerous move, but for a predator, control was everything. And Peter would risk it all to reclaim it.

Their bodies collided, and the struggle for the gun began immediately. Hands grappled, knuckles white as each fought for dominance.

Daniel's movements were swift and deliberate, the kind only a trained fighter possessed. He twisted, using Peter's momentum against him, but Peter held on, his fingers clawing at the gun's handle.

Claire was in shock as she watched the fight unfold. She knew Peter was formidable, but Daniel matched him blow for blow. Where did this come from? She couldn't reconcile this skilled fighter with the easygoing, carefree person she thought she knew. But then again, had she truly known Daniel at all?

A sudden sharp metallic clatter pierced the air as the weapon slipped from Daniel's grasp, skidding across the floor and disappearing into the shadows.

Without the gun, the two men collided in a violent tangle of limbs, each fighting to gain the upper hand. Their struggle tore through crates, scattering tools and debris across the floor.

Peter's raw aggression met Daniel's practiced skill head-on. Fists slammed into flesh, bodies crashed against metal and wood, and the air pulsed with the sickening thuds of hits finding their mark.

Then, the door burst open again, and Carl stormed in, his face contorted with a mix of shock and fury at the sight of the melee. Without hesitation, he charged toward Daniel.

Claire could only watch in horror. Two against one—did Daniel stand a chance?

But to her surprise, Daniel closed the gap with startling speed. His fist shot out, connecting with Carl's jaw. The impact sent Carl stumbling back, blood bubbling at the corner of his mouth.

It happened so fast that Peter could barely react. Daniel spun on him, his fist driving into Peter's ribs with savage ferocity. A startled gasp escaped Peter as he doubled over, the air punched from his lungs.

Carl let out an enraged roar and charged at Daniel again, but Daniel ducked, countered, and sent Carl crashing to the ground.

"Claire!" Daniel's scream burst through the chaos. "Get the gun!"

His command snapped her from her stupor. Frantically scanning the dusty floor, she saw a flash of metal by the back wall.

But Peter, now recovered from Daniel's brutal gut punch, saw it too.

A desperate race began.

Her heart thundered as she crawled toward the weapon, fingers stretching—

She snatched it just in time, her hand closing around the gun's handle. Cold. Heavy. Real. The weight of it sent a shiver through her hand.

She stood up and spun around, her chest heaving. "Don't come any closer," she warned, her voice quivering. "I d-don't want to shoot you...but I will."

Peter took a deliberate step forward. His smirk was cruel, taunting her.

The world around her blurred; all she could focus on was the weapon in her hand and the predator stalking closer.

Can I do it? The question flashed in her mind in an instant. *Can I pull the trigger if it comes to that?*

She tried to steady her grip, but her fingers shook uncontrollably.

Peter must have seen it. He read the hesitation in her hands, the fear in her eyes, like a predator sensing weakness.

With a sudden, vicious movement, he charged at her.

Time fractured. One moment, Peter's vicious face filled her vision; the next, a guttural roar shattered the air, like a wounded animal in its final fight.

Jack hurled himself at Peter, pouring every last ounce of strength into the attack. Blood streaked down his temple, his face convulsing in agony. His strength defied reason, his body a weapon fueled by love and desperation.

The floor shuddered beneath the impact as Jack drove Peter to the ground.

With his knee pressed into Peter's chest, Jack growled through gritted teeth, "Do. NOT. Touch. Her."

His tone was lethal—every syllable a promise wrapped in rage.

Peter lay motionless beneath him, his eyes glassy, his arrogance crushed beneath Jack's wrath.

Claire stood frozen, her fingers still clenched tightly around the gun.

Her gaze drifted to the far side of the shed, where Carl now lay sprawled motionless on the ground.

Before she could fully process the sight, Daniel's voice cut through the confusion.

"It appears both men are subdued," he announced, his voice unsettlingly composed. "I need you to give me the gun."

Claire whipped her head toward him. He stood beside her, his hand extended calmly, his green eyes locked into hers.

But despite his steady demeanor, the dark bruise already forming above his left eyebrow told the true story of the chaos that had just unfolded.

"Give you the gun?" Her voice was sharp, suspicion twisting through every word.

Instead of handing it over, her fingers tightened around the cold, unforgiving metal. She couldn't let it go—not yet.

Daniel had found her. Fought for her. Saved her.

But what if his heroism was all an act? What if giving up the weapon meant surrendering her only chance at survival?

Her pulse pounded in her ears, a relentless drumbeat of doubt.

She wanted to believe in him, to let the gun slip from her hand.

But every instinct screamed at her to hold on to it.

Trust no one.

Not even the man whose bravery might be nothing but a façade.

Chapter 38

Daniel's Revelation

The room seemed to hold its breath, each second stretching into an agonizing eternity. Daniel's expression was carved with concern—but couldn't it just as easily be a mask of deceit?

Claire's hand shook violently, her knuckles turning white against the hard steel of the gun. It was her last leverage, the only thing keeping her and Jack alive.

"Why should I hand it over?" she demanded, her voice defiant.

Daniel raised an eyebrow, then let out a long, weary sigh. Whether it was a smirk threatening to break through or sheer exhaustion settling in, Claire couldn't tell. His hand remained outstretched, steady and unyielding.

"Claire," he replied finally, his voice calm, "I know you're scared and probably don't trust me right now, but I literally just saved your life. I'd think that's reason enough to give it to me." His gaze dropped to her trembling hand. "Also, because your hand is shaking so much, I'm pretty sure you're about to shoot someone...and I'd prefer it *not* be me."

Looking into Daniel's eyes, she saw only sincerity and compassion. But it was the unwavering calm, devoid of any deception or cruelty that made her want to believe him.

All the fight within her dissipated, her resistance finally burning itself out. Her fingers loosened, and the weapon slipped from her grasp into his waiting hand.

Daniel accepted it carefully as Jack staggered toward them, his face pale and drawn. The strength that had driven him moments ago was now gone, leaving him barely able to hold himself upright.

Claire instinctively wrapped her arm around him, steadying him the best she could. His body swayed against her. Too weak. Too much blood lost.

"I never wanted it to come to this," Daniel uttered, his voice heavy with regret as his gaze took in Jack and Claire's battered state. Turning to Claire, he said, "I've been so worried about you."

The words, meant to soothe, felt like a fresh wound. After everything he'd put them through—he was worried?

"Are you kidding?" she snapped, heat surging back into her veins. "This is all *your* fault! You're the one who arranged that meeting. You're the one who tried to buy an illegal tusk!"

Guilt flickered in Daniel's expression. "Claire, I know. This is on me. I should have seen it coming. I should have kept you safe." His eyes locked onto hers, a silent plea. "But buying the tusk was the only way to gain Miller's trust."

Then he dropped the bombshell, his next words shattering everything Claire thought she knew.

"Claire, I'm not even a student. I was assigned to the college as an undercover agent working with Kenya's Anti-Poaching Unit."

"What?" The word slipped from her lips as her mind struggled to process what he was saying.

"They suspected someone on campus was part of a major poaching ring, but I had no idea it was Miller—not at first."

His voice faltered, every word threaded with a deep need for her to understand. "Then you were so brave and captured our meeting on your phone. I was going to tell you everything the next day because I couldn't bear lying to you anymore. But you disappeared."

A shadow of pain crossed his face. "You trusted the one person I suspected most—Peter Miller, if that's even his real name."

Claire's world tilted, reality splintering under the weight of the truth. Daniel wasn't the villain—he was the hero. The one who had been working all along to dismantle the very danger that had upended her life.

Her mind raced, trying to piece it together. How had she not seen it?

"You were never a student?" Claire's voice shook. "You were just pretending the whole time?"

His expression was steady, almost pained. "Well, yes," he said, his voice low but direct. "Even the professors didn't know. Only the Dean knew who I really was. The rest...that was all part of the mission."

A dozen memories flashed through her mind: his easy laugh, the late-night study sessions, the quiet moments when he'd listened—really listened. The way his expression softened when she spoke about her brother, the compassion in his eyes.

The warmth of those moments was suddenly overshadowed by doubt. Had it all been an act?

Her voice barely rose above a whisper as she asked, "What about our friendship? Was *that* real?"

Daniel's expression softened, a genuine warmth shining through. "The time I spent with you and Rachel was...well, the best time of my life," he confessed. "I always knew my assignment, but I never expected to form such close friendships. I never expected to care this much."

His voice dropped, a raw ache threading through his words. "When you vanished, Claire, it ripped me apart. I thought I lost you..." His voice cracked, and a faint sheen glistened in his eyes. "You can't imagine my shock," he continued, "when I followed Miller to this shed and found you inside. It felt like a miracle—a terrifying, impossible miracle."

Claire didn't think—she just moved. She closed the space between them, wrapping her arm around him. His body stiffened for just a moment, then melted into a strong embrace, his breath hitching against her shoulder.

His next words were barely more than a whisper. "Where have you been all this time?"

Reluctantly, Claire stepped back, her fingers lingering on his arm as if afraid to break the fragile connection. She swallowed hard, choking back the tears that threatened to spill over.

When she spoke, the words tumbled out in a breathless rush—her abduction, the desperate chase through the savanna, her injuries, and finding sanctuary at the orphanage with Jack.

Then Jack spoke up, his voice a thin, brittle whisper. "We came back... for the photo on her flash drive. We thought... it was the key... to taking them down."

A fierce, righteous fury blazed across Daniel's face, his voice rolling like thunder as he looked at Peter. "You're a cold-hearted monster, Miller."

Peter didn't respond. He remained motionless, his chest rising and falling in shallow, feeble rhythms.

"We need to tie these two up," Daniel urged.

"But what about Johnny?" Claire asked, rummaging through the debris for rope.

"I already took care of him. But once we're done, we need to get Jack to a doctor. He's lost too much blood."

Jack's knees suddenly buckled, his body swaying as if the ground had shifted beneath him.

"Let's sit him down before he collapses," Daniel insisted.

As they guided Jack onto a crate, Peter seized his opportunity. He sprang to his feet, hurling himself at Daniel and the gun.

A life-or-death struggle erupted, savage and chaotic. In a desperate move, Peter's hand closed around the gun, his fingers clawing at the metal as he tried to wrench it from Daniel's grip.

A scream ripped from Claire's throat as she watched them. If Peter gained control of the weapon, it would mean the end of them all.

She wanted to move, to help. But fear anchored her to the

spot.

Then the gun discharged with a booming *crack.*

The shot exploded through the tiny shed, sending shockwaves through Claire's entire body. Her bones felt like they might shatter under the force.

Peter staggered. His blue eyes locked onto Claire's—a fleeting, desperate connection. Then his body crumpled to the ground with a sickening thud.

Claire stood paralyzed, horror coursing through her as a steady stream of blood began to pool beneath him, crimson and final.

Daniel rushed forward, dropping to his knees. His fingers pressed against Peter's neck, searching. Then, a slow shake of his head.

"He's gone."

The words hit her like a crashing wave, leaving her gasping for air. But there was no time to absorb the truth of it.

"Claire!" Daniel yelled. "Carl's waking up! I need something to tie him up!"

In a desperate dash, Claire found a coil of rope and thrust it into Daniel's hands. His movements were swift as he secured the knots tightly.

Then a strangled groan pierced the shed. They turned just in time to see Jack's eyes roll back, his body collapsing to the ground.

"Jack!" Claire screamed as she dropped to his side, her hand wrapping around his too-cold fingers.

"Daniel, help him!" she cried out, her voice cracking under the strain of fear.

Daniel darted over, kneeling beside him. Daniel's hands moved quickly, checking Jack's pulse, his pupils, his breathing.

"He needs a doctor. *Now!*"

In one swift motion, Daniel scooped Jack up, hoisting him effortlessly over his broad shoulder.

"Follow me!" he yelled, bolting out of the shed.

Claire staggered to her feet, her vision swimming with

tears. She somehow forced her legs to move and began to run after Daniel.

The blood staining her hands felt insignificant compared to the terror gripping her heart. Jack, the man she loved, hung limp over Daniel's shoulder, his life ebbing away with every stride.

She sprinted through the campus...a desperate plea trapped in her throat.

God, save him!

Every second was an enemy, each tick of the clock a brutal, relentless countdown—

And time was running out.

Chapter 39

The Aftermath

As Claire sank into her window seat, the low hum of the engines vibrated through her, matching the pounding in her temples.

The fiberglass cast on her arm—lighter, less restrictive than the sling that once confined her—rested against her lap, a tangible reminder of all that had happened in Kenya.

Four weeks had passed since the terrifying showdown in the maintenance shed, yet its weight still pressed against her heart.

Twelve hours to Paris. A layover. Then another eight hours to Philadelphia. The journey home felt as daunting as the memories she had spent weeks trying to outrun.

Jack's fight for survival loomed most vividly, sending a shiver through her.

The frantic race to the hospital played like a reel in her mind, like it had happened only yesterday.

"Claire, keep talking to him!" Daniel's voice had been taut with urgency as they sped down the uneven Kenyan roads. "Don't let him drift off!"

She had clutched Jack's hand, her voice barely holding together. "Jack, stay with me. Please. You're going to be okay."

His eyelids fluttered, his voice barely a whisper. "I... promised...to protect you."

A sob broke from her throat. "You did protect me." She

squeezed his fingers. "Now it's my turn."

When they finally reached the hospital, she could do nothing but watch helplessly as Jack was rushed through the doors.

The hours of waiting were agonizing.

When his eyes finally opened, relief flooded her so powerfully that she collapsed into the chair beside him, sobbing.

"Hey," he rasped weakly, offering her the faintest smile. "I'm not going anywhere."

She laughed through her tears, clutching his hand. "Don't scare me like that again."

The days that followed merged into a blur of sleepless nights and slow healing.

Claire's parents arrived at the hospital just as the dust was settling, and they never left her side. For weeks, they prayed with her, comforted her, and reminded her she was not alone.

Though shattered by the pain she had endured, they were profoundly grateful for the miracle of her survival.

Justice, swift and necessary, soon followed. Johnny and Carl, along with the red-haired accomplice, were apprehended and charged with attempted murder.

At the college, Peter's network began to unravel. Samuel, the corrupt guard, was detained. Others were identified. Once a pawn in their deadly game, Claire emerged as the victor, playing a crucial role in their eventual downfall.

Peter Miller, whose real name was Peter Constantine, was unmasked as a notorious poacher. He fled to Kenya to evade his criminal past, adopting a false identity in order to exploit Africa's most endangered wildlife.

His death was ruled self-defense. Yet, the memory of his lifeless body continued to haunt Claire's dreams. His piercing blue eyes—forever dimmed.

"I didn't want this," she had confessed to Daniel during the inquest. They sat in a quiet courthouse hallway. "Even after everything, I didn't want him to die."

Daniel had placed a hand on her shoulder. "None of us did.

But Peter made his choices. And if given the chance, he would have killed every person in that shed."

The truth in Daniel's words gave her the strength to endure the hearings.

Rachel traveled from the campus to offer her support. She sat with Claire every evening, sometimes speaking, sometimes simply offering the comfort of silence. Their friendship deepened in those days, strengthened as they navigated the ordeal together.

A week into Jack's recovery, Sadie arrived, bringing warmth and laughter back to his hospital room. She burst in, her arms overflowing with handmade cards.

"These are from the kiddos. They wanted to make sure you knew they're rooting for you."

Jack flipped through the colorful, scrawled messages, his words tangling in his throat. "This…this means a lot."

Sadie beamed. "Oh! And guess what? A local pastor has agreed to take over at the orphanage until you're back on your feet."

Claire hugged her tightly. "Thank you, Sadie. For everything."

Each person—her parents, her friends, even the kind strangers who helped her through the darkest moments—had been placed in her life at exactly the right time.

She saw God's hand in it all.

And she was grateful.

Now, four weeks later, the time had come to leave Kenya.

The goodbyes were a tangled mix of sadness and hope. She assured all her friends that their paths would cross again someday.

But the hardest farewell had been at Jack's bedside that morning—a goodbye that left a deep ache.

"I can't believe you're really leaving," he had muttered, his voice thick with emotion.

"You know I can't stay, Jack," she had told him, her voice a whisper. "I have to finish college, and you'll be heading back to the orphanage soon. But I'll find my way back to you. I...I promise."

His lips had curved into a bittersweet smile as he pulled her into his arms, enveloping her as if letting go might break something.

"I'll hold you to that," he whispered.

And when the door clicked shut behind her, she felt like her heart had split in two. Even as she vowed to return to him, she doubted her own words.

Their paths were pulling them in opposite directions, with thousands of miles stretching between them, a chasm that felt too wide to overcome.

A silent question hung over their future, and she couldn't help but wonder if their love could survive the distance.

The plane's sudden lurch roused her from her reverie. Claire closed her eyes, inhaling deeply. She reminded herself that God was weaving an intricate plan for her life, a tapestry of beauty and purpose she couldn't yet fully see.

Her journey wasn't ending. It was just shifting.

As the aircraft roared down the runway, she let go of the uncertainties and surrendered the unknown future into God's loving hands.

Soon, the tension in her temples began to fade.

As the African landscape shrank beneath her, she felt a quiet strength rising within her.

She was ready.

Ready to face whatever came next.

Ready to go home.

Chapter 40

Return to Kenya

As the bus rumbled along the dusty Kenyan road, every jolt and bump stirred memories of Claire's first wild journey into this untamed land.

But this time, it was different.

She sat comfortably near the front, a far cry from the chaotic, bone-jarring ride she'd endured before.

Just then, the bus jolted violently over a deep crater, sending the passengers in the backseat airborne.

A wry smile tugged at her lips. "Well," she murmured, "some things never change."

The intercom crackled to life. "Next stop, fifteen minutes!" the driver announced.

Outside the window, the golden savanna stretched endlessly beneath a cloudless sky. The land was just as wild, just as unforgiving, and just as breathtaking as she remembered.

And yet, everything had changed.

Two years had passed since her first trip to Kenya, a scorching trial by fire that had shaped her in ways she was only beginning to understand.

The wounds from that terrifying ordeal had softened over time, leaving behind a resilient strength she never imagined she possessed.

Her faith, once shaken to its core, had been rebuilt, stronger and more resolute. And now, it had led her back here.

The low hum of the bus lulled Claire into quiet reflection, her thoughts drifting back to the months following her return home.

"You're stronger than you realize, Claire," Rachel had affirmed one evening as they sat on her couch, steaming cups of tea in hand. "You've survived things most people can't even imagine. Lean into God's strength. He'll carry you through this."

Claire's reunion with Rachel had come earlier than expected. As soon as the semester had ended, Rachel boarded a flight to Philadelphia, skipping California entirely.

And then a few days later, Daniel joined them.

Fresh from wrapping up his undercover assignment, he filled her apartment with booming laughter and exaggerated stories, spinning even the most harrowing events into ridiculous adventures.

The three of them, inseparable once again, reminded Claire of who she was before the fear, before the scars. And for the first time in a long time, she felt like herself again.

A few months later, Claire traveled to Georgia to celebrate Mark's cancer-free diagnosis with Sadie.

"I can't believe it," Sadie whispered through tears, pulling her into a strong embrace. "We've been given a second chance."

It was a moment of pure joy—a powerful reminder of life's fragile blessings and the countless gifts she had been given.

And through it all, there was Jack. The man who stole her heart and never let it go.

Not a single day had passed without a phone call, a message, a promise that he was waiting for her.

"You wouldn't believe what the kids did today," he would say, telling her stories of the orphans' antics.

And always, he ended with, "You should be here, Claire."

A year later, he made sure she was.

On her graduation day, Claire stepped onto the stage—and there he was—sitting proudly beside her parents, beaming with that familiar, unwavering love in his eyes.

Then came the day she would never forget.

At the Philadelphia Zoo, standing in front of the African animal exhibit, Jack dropped to one knee.

"Claire, we've faced more together than most couples do in a lifetime," he declared, grinning at her. "Honestly, if we've survived all that, marriage should be a walk in the park."

Then, holding out the ring, he asked, "Will you marry me?"

She laughed, cried, and said yes all at once.

A small chuckle escaped her at the memory, catching the attention of a curious fellow passenger. Still smiling, Claire shifted her gaze to the Kenyan landscape rolling past her window.

And now, I'm back.

Six months of fundraising, planning, and prayers had brought her to this moment. As the newest missionary at The House of Hope, she was eager to serve.

A voice pulled her from her thoughts. "Hey Claire, we're here," the girl beside her announced as they arrived at the orphanage gate.

She met Rachel's cheerful face, and a rush of happiness blanketed her.

Claire turned to the couple behind her. "Mom and Dad—Jack should be waiting for us at the entrance."

Her parents' faces shone with pride and affection as they gathered their belongings.

As the bus slowed to a stop, she reached out for Rachel's hand, her voice barely above a whisper.

"I can't believe this is real," she said, a nervous flutter rising in her stomach. "We're finally here…and I'm about to get married."

"Of course, it's real!" Rachel grinned. "I flew halfway across the world to be your maid-of-honor, so this wedding is happening!" She squeezed Claire's hand. "You and Jack are meant to be together, and those orphans…they're going to be so blessed to have you."

Tears pricked Claire's eyes as she squeezed Rachel's hand in return. "Thank you."

The gate swung open, and the bus rumbled into the orphanage grounds. The familiar surroundings and the joyous shouts of children greeted Claire like an old friend.

"Don't forget your camera!" Daniel chimed in, retrieving her camera bag wedged between the seats. "And try not to let it get destroyed this time!"

"Thanks, Daniel," she laughed as she slipped the bag over her shoulder.

With her new camera in hand and the people she cherished most gathered around her, Claire stepped off the bus. The world stretched before her—a vast canvas waiting to be captured, each frame a story waiting to be told.

With a joyous laugh, she dashed toward the brown-eyed missionary waiting near the steps, his arms open wide.

She flew into his embrace, his hold gentle yet steadfast, a safe harbor filled with love. She clung to him, happiness bubbling up through her tears.

And in that moment, she knew that her past was no longer a burden to bear. It was a thread woven into something greater—a tapestry of pain, faith, and healing that had brought her here.

This wasn't just where she belonged.

It was home.

About The Author

Shannon Bernard

Shannon Bernard is a retired English teacher, devoted wife, and mother of three. With a wealth of experiences from her travels abroad, she infuses her storytelling with depth and authenticity.

Inspired by her mother, who founded an orphanage in Kenya, Shannon has journeyed across Africa, ministering to children and witnessing life's raw beauty and challenges firsthand. From daily life at the orphanage to treating the eye infections of Maasai children and narrowly escaping an elephant attack, her experiences breathe vivid realism into her novel, making every detail resonate with authenticity and heart

Books By This Author

Journey Of Hope

Journey of Hope follows Emma as she embarks on a personal quest to China in search of her biological family and a deeper connection to her heritage. But what begins as a journey of self-discovery quickly spirals into a whirlwind of mistaken identities, enigmatic strangers, and a desperate chase involving orphaned baby girls and relentless police pursuit. Thrust into danger, Emma finds an unlikely ally in a captivating young man whose motives remain shrouded in mystery. As trust becomes a matter of survival, she must determine whether he is her salvation—or her greatest threat. Along the way, Emma's faith is tested like never before, forcing her to confront the ultimate question: will she place her trust in man, or in the only One who truly holds her future?

Made in the USA
Middletown, DE
23 March 2025